# The First Men
# in the Moon

# BY THE SAME AUTHOR
## ALL PUBLISHED BY HOUSE OF STRATUS

# The First Men
# in the Moon

# H G WELLS

HOUSE OF
STRATUS

This edition published in 2002 by House of Stratus, an imprint of House of Stratus Ltd, Thirsk Industrial Park, York Road, Thirsk, North Yorkshire, YO7 3BX, UK.
Also at: House of Stratus Inc., 2 Neptune Road, Poughkeepsie, NY 12601, USA.

www.houseofstratus.com

Typeset, printed and bound by House of Stratus.

A catalogue record for this book is available from the British Library and The Library of Congress.

ISBN 0-7551-0401-3

# CONTENTS

# CHAPTER ONE

## Mr Bedford Meets Mr Cavor at Lympne

As I sit down to write here amidst the shadows of vine-leaves under the blue sky of southern Italy, it comes to me with a certain quality of astonishment that my participation in these amazing adventures of Mr Cavor was, after all, the outcome of the purest accident. It might have been any one. I fell into these things at a time when I thought myself removed from the slightest possibility of disturbing experiences. I had gone to Lympne because I had imagined it the most uneventful place in the world. "Here, at any rate," said I, "I shall find peace and a chance to work!"

And this book is the sequel. So utterly at variance is Destiny with all the little plans of men.

I may perhaps mention here that very recently I had come an ugly cropper in certain business enterprises. Sitting now surrounded by all the circumstances of wealth, there is a luxury in admitting my extremity. I can admit, even, that to a certain extent my disasters were conceivably of my own making. It may be there are directions in which I have some capacity, but the conduct of business operations is not among these. But in those days I was young, and my youth among other objectionable

1

forms took that of a pride in my capacity for affairs. I am young still in years, but the things that have happened to me have rubbed something of the youth from my mind. Whether they have brought any wisdom to light below it is a more doubtful matter.

It is scarcely necessary to go into the details of the speculations that landed me at Lympne, in Kent. Nowadays even about business transactions there is a strong spice of adventure. I took risks. In these things there is invariably a certain amount of give and take, and it fell to me finally to do the giving. Reluctantly enough. Even when I had got out of everything, one cantankerous creditor saw fit to be malignant. Perhaps you have met that flaming sense of outraged virtue, or perhaps you have only felt it. He ran me hard. It seemed to me, at last, that there was nothing for it but to write a play, unless I wanted to drudge for my living as a clerk. I have a certain imagination, and luxurious tastes, and I meant to make a vigorous fight for it before that fate overtook me. In addition to my belief in my powers as a businessman, I had always in those days had an idea that I was equal to writing a very good play. It is not, I believe, a very uncommon persuasion. I knew there is nothing a man can do outside legitimate business transactions that has such opulent possibilities, and very probably that biased my opinion. I had, indeed, got into the habit of regarding this unwritten drama as a convenient little reserve put by for a rainy day. That rainy day had come, and I set to work.

I soon discovered that writing a play was a longer business than I had supposed; at first I had reckoned ten days for it, and it was to have a *pied-a-terre* while it was in hand that I came to Lympne. I reckoned myself lucky in getting that little bungalow.

I got it on a three years' agreement. I put in a few sticks of furniture, and while the play was in hand I did my own cooking. My cooking would have shocked Mrs Bond. And yet, you know, it had flavour. I had a coffee-pot, a saucepan for eggs, and one for potatoes, and a frying pan for sausages and bacon – such was the simple apparatus of my comfort. One cannot always be magnificent, but simplicity is always a possible alternative. For the rest I laid in an eighteen-gallon cask of beer on credit, and a trustful baker came each day. It was not, perhaps, in the style of Sybaris, but I have had worse times. I was a little sorry for the baker, who was a very decent man indeed, but even for him I hoped.

Certainly if anyone wants solitude, the place is Lympne. It is in the clay part of Kent, and my bungalow stood on the edge of an old sea cliff and stared across the flats of Romney Marsh at the sea. In very wet weather the place is almost inaccessible, and I have heard that at times the postman used to traverse the more succulent portions of his route with boards upon his feet. I never saw him doing so, but I can quite imagine it. Outside the doors of the few cottages and houses that make up the present village big birch besoms are stuck, to wipe off the worst of the clay, which will give some idea of the texture of the district. I doubt if the place would be there at all, if it were not a fading memory of things gone for ever. It was the big port of England in Roman times, Portus Lemanus, and now the sea is four miles away. All down the steep hill are boulders and masses of Roman brickwork, and from it old Watling Street, still paved in places, starts like an arrow to the north. I used to stand on the hill and think of it all, the galleys and legions, the captives and officials, the women and traders, the speculators like myself, all the swarm

3

and tumult that came clanking in and out of the harbour. And now just a few lumps of rubble on a grassy slope, and a sheep or two – and me! And where the port had been were the levels of the marsh, sweeping round in a broad curve to distant Dungeness, and dotted here and there with tree clumps and the church towers of old mediaeval towns that are following Lemanus now towards extinction.

That outlook on the marsh was, indeed, one of the finest views I have ever seen. I suppose Dungeness was fifteen miles away; it lay like a raft on the sea, and farther westward were the hills by Hastings under the setting sun. Sometimes they hung close and clear, sometimes they were faded and low, and often the drift of the weather took them clean out of sight. And all the nearer parts of the marsh were laced and lit by ditches and canals.

The window at which I worked looked over the skyline of this crest, and it was from this window that I first set eyes on Cavor. It was just as I was struggling with my scenario, holding down my mind to the sheer hard work of it, and naturally enough he arrested my attention.

The sun had set, the sky was a vivid tranquillity of green and yellow, and against that he came out black – the oddest little figure.

He was a short, round-bodied, thin-legged little man, with a jerky quality in his motions; he had seen fit to clothe his extraordinary mind in a cricket cap, an overcoat, and cycling knickerbockers and stockings. Why he did so I do not know, for he never cycled and he never played cricket. It was a fortuitous concurrence of garments, arising I know not how. He gesticulated with his hands and arms, and jerked his head about and *buzzed*. He buzzed like something electric. You never heard such buzzing. And ever and again he cleared his throat with a most extraordinary noise.

There had been rain, and that spasmodic walk of his was enhanced by the extreme slipperiness of the footpath. Exactly as he came against the sun he stopped, pulled out a watch, hesitated. Then with a sort of convulsive gesture he turned and retreated with every manifestation of haste, no longer gesticulating, but going with ample strides that showed the relatively large size of his feet – they were, I remember, grotesquely exaggerated in size by adhesive clay – to the best possible advantage.

This occurred on the first day of my sojourn, when my play-writing energy was at its height and I regarded the incident simply as an annoying distraction – the waste of five minutes. I returned to my scenario. But when next evening the apparition was repeated with remarkable precision, and again the next evening, and indeed every evening when rain was not falling, concentration upon the scenario became a considerable effort. "Confound the man," I said, "one would think he was learning to be a marionette!" and for several evenings I cursed him pretty heartily.

Then my annoyance gave way to amazement and curiosity. Why on earth should a man do this thing? On the fourteenth evening I could stand it no longer, and so soon as he appeared I opened the french window, crossed the verandah, and directed myself to the point where he invariably stopped.

He had his watch out as I came up to him. He had a chubby, rubicund face with reddish brown eyes – previously I had seen him only against the light. "One moment, sir," said I as he turned.

He stared. "One moment," he said, "certainly. Or if you wish to speak to me for longer, and it is not asking too much – your moment is up – would it trouble you to accompany me?"

"Not in the least," said I, placing myself beside him.

"My habits are regular. My time for intercourse – limited."

"This, I presume, is your time for exercise?"

"It is. I come here to enjoy the sunset."

"You don't."

"Sir?"

"You never look at it."

"Never look at it?"

"No. I've watched you thirteen nights, and not once have you looked at the sunset – not once."

He knitted his brows like one who encounters a problem.

"Well, I enjoy the sunlight – the atmosphere – I go along this path, through that gate" – he jerked his head over his shoulder – "and round – "

"You don't. You never have been. It's all nonsense. There isn't a way. Tonight for instance – "

"Oh! tonight! Let me see. Ah! I just glanced at my watch, saw that I had already been out just three minutes over the precise half-hour, decided there was not time to go round, turned – "

"You always do."

He looked at me – reflected. "Perhaps I do, now I come to think of it. But what was it you wanted to speak to me about?"

"Why, this!"

"This?"

"Yes. Why do you do it? Every night you come making a noise – "

"Making a noise?"

6

"Like this" – I imitated his buzzing noise.

He looked at me, and it was evident the buzzing awakened distaste. "Do I do *that?*" he asked.

"Every blessed evening."

"I had no idea."

He stopped dead. He regarded me gravely. "Can it be," he said, "that I have formed a Habit?"

"Well, it looks like it. Doesn't it?"

He pulled down his lower lip between finger and thumb. He regarded a puddle at his feet.

"My mind is much occupied," he said. "And you want to know *why!* Well, sir, I can assure you that not only do I not know why I do these things, but I did not even know I did them. Come to think, it is just as you say; I never *have* been beyond that field... And these things annoy you?"

For some reason I was beginning to relent towards him. "Not *annoy*," I said. "But – imagine yourself writing a play!"

"I couldn't."

"Well, anything that needs concentration."

"Ah!" he said, "of course," and meditated. His expression became so eloquent of distress, that I relented still more. After all, there *is* a touch of aggression in demanding of a man you don't know why he hums on a public footpath.

"You see," he said weakly, "it's a habit."

"Oh, I recognise that."

"I must stop it."

"But not if it puts you out. After all, I had no business – it's something of a liberty."

"Not at all, sir," he said, "not at all. I am greatly indebted to you. I should guard myself against these things. In future I will. Could I trouble you – once again? That noise?"

"Something like this," I said. "Zuzzoo, zuzzoo. But really, you know – "

"I am greatly obliged to you. In fact, I know I am getting absurdly absent-minded. You are quite justified, sir – perfectly justified. Indeed, I am indebted to you. The thing shall end. And now, sir, I have already brought you farther than I should have done."

"I do hope my impertinence – "

"Not at all, sir, not at all."

We regarded each other for a moment. I raised my hat and wished him a good evening. He responded convulsively, and so we went our ways.

At the stile I looked back at his receding figure. His bearing had changed remarkably, he seemed limp, shrunken. The contrast with his former gesticulating, zuzzoing self took me in some absurd way as pathetic. I watched him out of sight. Then wishing very heartily I had kept to my own business, I returned to my bungalow and my play.

The next evening I saw nothing of him, nor the next. But he was very much in my mind, and it had occurred to me that as a sentimental comic character he might serve a useful purpose in the development of my plot.

The third day he called upon me.

For a time I was puzzled to think what had brought him. He made indifferent conversation in the most formal way, then abruptly he came to business. He wanted to buy me out of my bungalow.

"You see," he said, "I don't blame you in the least, but you've destroyed a habit, and it disorganises my day. I've walked past here for years – years. No doubt I've hummed... You've made all that impossible!"

I suggested he might try some other direction.

"No. There is no other direction. This is the only one. I've inquired. And now – every afternoon at four – I come to a dead wall."

"But, my dear sir, if the thing is so important to you..."

"It's vital. You see, I'm – I'm an investigator – I am engaged in a scientific research. I live – " he paused and seemed to think. "Just over there," he said, and pointed suddenly dangerously near my eye. "The house with white chimneys you see just over the trees. And my circumstances are abnormal – abnormal. I am on the point of completing one of the most important – demonstrations – I can assure you one of *the most important* demonstrations that have ever been made. It requires constant thought, constant mental ease and activity. And the afternoon was my brightest time! – effervescing with new ideas – new points of view."

"But why not come by still?"

"It would be all different. I should be self-conscious. I should think of you at your play – watching me irritated – instead of thinking of my work. No! I must have the bungalow."

I meditated. Naturally, I wanted to think the matter over thoroughly before anything decisive was said. I was generally ready enough for business in those days, and selling always attracted me; but in the first place it was not my bungalow, and even if I sold it to him at a good price I might get inconvenienced in the delivery of goods if the current owner got wind of the transaction, and in the second I was, well – undischarged. It was clearly a business that required delicate handling. Moreover, the possibility of his being in pursuit of some valuable invention also interested me. It occurred to me that I would like to know more of this research, not with any dishonest intention, but simply with an idea that to know what it was would be a relief from play-writing. I threw out feelers.

He was quite willing to supply information. Indeed, once he was fairly under way the conversation became a monologue. He talked like a man long pent up, who has had it over with himself again and again. He talked for nearly an hour, and I must confess I found it a pretty stiff bit of listening. But through it all there was the undertone of satisfaction one feels when one is neglecting work one has set oneself. During that first interview I gathered very little of the drift of his work. Half his words were technicalities entirely strange to me, and he illustrated one or two points with what he was pleased to call elementary mathematics, computing on an envelope with a copying-ink pencil, in a manner that made it hard even to seem to understand. "Yes," I said, "yes. Go on!" Nevertheless I made out enough to convince me that he was no mere crank playing at discoveries. In spite of his crank-like appearance there was a force about him that made that impossible. Whatever it was, it was a thing with mechanical possibilities. He told me of a work-shed he had, and of three assistants – originally jobbing carpenters – whom he had trained. Now, from the work-shed to the patent office is clearly only one step. He invited me to see those things. I accepted readily, and took care, by a remark or so, to underline that. The proposed transfer of the bungalow remained very conveniently in suspense.

At last he rose to depart, with an apology for the length of his call. Talking over his work was, he said, a pleasure enjoyed only too rarely. It was not often he found such an intelligent listener as myself, he mingled very little with professional scientific men.

"So much pettiness," he explained; "so much intrigue! And really, when one has an idea – a novel, fertilising idea – I don't want to be uncharitable, but – "

I am a man who believes in impulses. I made what was perhaps a rash proposition. But you must remember, that I had been alone, play-writing in Lympne, for fourteen days, and my compunction for his ruined walk still hung about me. "Why not," said I, "make this your new habit? In the place of the one I spoilt? At least, until we can settle about the bungalow. What you want is to turn over your work in your mind. That you have always done during your afternoon walk. Unfortunately that's over – you can't get things back as they were. But why not come and talk about your work to me; use me as a sort of wall against which you may throw your thoughts and catch them again? It's certain I don't know enough to steal your ideas myself – and I know no scientific men – "

I stopped. He was considering. Evidently the thing, attracted him. "But I'm afraid I should bore you," he said.

"You think I'm too dull?"

"Oh, no; but technicalities – "

"Anyhow, you've interested me immensely this afternoon."

"Of course it *would* be a great help to me. Nothing clears up one's ideas so much as explaining them. Hitherto – "

"My dear sir, say no more."

"But really can you spare the time?"

"There is no rest like change of occupation," I said, with profound conviction.

The affair was over. On my verandah steps he turned. "I am already greatly indebted to you," he said.

I made an interrogative noise.

"You have completely cured me of that ridiculous habit of humming," he explained.

I think I said I was glad to be of any service to him, and he turned away.

Immediately the train of thought that our conversation had suggested must have resumed its sway. His arms began to wave in their former fashion. The faint echo of "zuzzoo" came back to me on the breeze…

Well, after all, that was not my affair…

He came the next day, and again the next day after that, and delivered two lectures on physics to our mutual satisfaction. He talked with an air of being extremely lucid about the "ether" and "tubes of force," and "gravitational potential," and things like that, and I sat in my other folding-chair and said, "Yes," "Go on," "I follow you," to keep him going. It was tremendously difficult stuff, but I do not think he ever suspected how much I did not understand him. There were moments when I doubted whether I was well employed, but at any rate I was resting from that confounded play. Now and then things gleamed on me clearly for a space, only to vanish just when I thought I had hold of them. Sometimes my attention failed altogether, and I would give it up and sit and stare at him, wondering whether, after all, it would not be better to use him as a central figure in a good farce and let all this other stuff slide. And then, perhaps, I would catch on again for a bit.

At the earliest opportunity I went to see his house. It was large and carelessly furnished; there were no servants other than his three assistants, and his dietary and private life were characterised by a philosophical simplicity. He was a water-drinker, a vegetarian, and all those logical disciplinary things. But the sight of his equipment settled many doubts. It looked like business from cellar to attic – an amazing little place to find in an out-of-the-way village. The ground-floor rooms contained benches and apparatus, the bakehouse and scullery boiler had developed into respectable furnaces, dynamos occupied the cellar, and there was a gasometer in the garden. He showed it to me with all the confiding zest of a man who has been living too much alone. His seclusion was overflowing now in an excess of confidence, and I had the good luck to be the recipient.

The three assistants were creditable specimens of the class of "handy-men" from which they came. Conscientious if un-intelligent, strong, civil, and willing. One, Spargus, who did the cooking and all the metal work, had been a sailor; a second, Gibbs, was a joiner; and the third was an ex-jobbing gardener, and now general assistant. They were the merest labourers. All the intelligent work was done by Cavor. Theirs was the darkest ignorance compared even with my muddled impression.

And now, as to the nature of these inquiries. Here, unhappily, comes a grave difficulty. I am no scientific expert, and if I were to attempt to set forth in the highly scientific language of Mr Cavor the aim to which his experiments tended, I am afraid I should confuse not only the reader but myself, and almost certainly I should make some blunder that would bring upon me the mockery of every up-to-date student of mathematical physics in the country. The best thing I can do therefore is, I think to give my impressions in my own inexact language, without any attempt to wear a garment of knowledge to which I have no claim.

The object of Mr Cavor's search was a substance that should be "opaque" – he used some other word I have forgotten, but "opaque" conveys the idea – to "all forms of radiant energy." "Radiant energy," he made me understand, was anything like light or heat, or those Röntgen Rays there was so much talk about a year or so ago, or the electric waves of Marconi, or gravitation. All these things, he said, *radiate* out from centres, and act on bodies at a distance, whence comes the term "radiant energy." Now almost all substances are opaque to some form or other of radiant energy. Glass, for example, is transparent to light, but much less so to heat, so that it is useful as a fire-screen; and alum is transparent to light, but blocks heat completely. A solution of iodine in carbon bisulphide, on the other hand, completely blocks light, but is quite transparent to heat. It will hide a fire from you, but permit all its warmth to reach you. Metals are not only opaque to light and heat, but also to electrical energy, which passes through both iodine solution and glass almost as though they were not interposed. And so on.

Now all known substances are "transparent" to gravitation. You can use screens of various sorts to cut off the light or heat, or electrical influence of the sun, or the warmth of the earth from anything; you can screen things by sheets of metal from Marconi's rays, but nothing will cut off the gravitational attraction of the sun or the gravitational attraction of the earth. Yet why there should be nothing is hard to say. Cavor did not see why such a substance should not exist, and certainly I could not tell him. I had never thought of such a possibility before. He showed me by calculations on paper, which Lord Kelvin, no doubt, or Professor Lodge, or Professor Karl Pearson, or any of those great scientific people might have understood, but which simply reduced me to a hopeless muddle, that not only was such a substance possible, but that it must satisfy certain conditions. It was an amazing piece of reasoning. Much as it amazed and exercised me at the time, it would be impossible to reproduce it here. "Yes," I said to it all, "yes; go on!" Suffice it for this story that he believed he might be able to manufacture this possible substance opaque to gravitation out of a complicated alloy of metals and something new – a new element. I fancy – called, I believe, *helium*, which was sent to him from London in sealed stone jars. Doubt has been thrown upon this detail, but I am almost certain it was *helium* he had sent him in sealed stone jars. It was certainly something very gaseous and thin. If only I had taken notes...

But then, how was I to foresee the necessity of taking notes?

Anyone with the merest germ of an imagination will understand the extraordinary possibilities of such a substance, and will sympathise a little with the emotion I felt as this understanding emerged from the haze of abstruse phrases in which Cavor expressed himself. Comic relief in a play indeed! It was some time before I would believe that I had interpreted him aright, and I was very careful not to ask questions that would have enabled him to gauge the profundity of misunderstanding into which he dropped his daily exposition. But no one reading the story of it here will sympathise fully, because from my barren narrative it will be impossible to gather the strength of my conviction that this astonishing substance was positively going to be made.

I do not recall that I gave my play an hour's consecutive work at any time after my visit to his house. My imagination had other things to do. There seemed no limit to the possibilities of the stuff; whichever way I tried I came on miracles and revolutions. For example, if one wanted to lift a weight, however enormous, one had only to get a sheet of this substance beneath it, and one might lift it with a straw. My first natural impulse was to apply this principle to guns and ironclads, and all the material and methods of war, and from that to shipping, locomotion, building, every conceivable form of human industry. The chance that had brought me into the very birth-chamber of this new time – it was an epoch, no less – was one of those chances that come once in a thousand years. The thing unrolled, it expanded and expanded. Among other things I saw in it my redemption as a businessman. I saw a parent company, and daughter companies, applications to right of us, applications to left, rings and trusts, privileges, and concessions spreading and spreading, until one vast, stupendous Cavorite company ran and ruled the world.

And I was in it!

I took my line straight away. I knew I was staking everything, but I jumped there and then.

"We're on absolutely the biggest thing that has ever been invented," I said, and put the accent on "we." "If you want to keep me out of this, you'll have to do it with a gun. I'm coming down to be your fourth labourer tomorrow."

He seemed surprised at my enthusiasm, but not a bit suspicious or hostile. Rather, he was self-depreciatory.

He looked at me doubtfully. "But do you really think – ?" he said. "And your play! How about that play?"

"It's vanished!" I cried. "My dear sir, don't you see what you've got? Don't you see what you're going to do?"

That was merely a rhetorical turn, but positively, he didn't. At first I could not believe it. He had not had the beginning of the inkling of an idea. This astonishing little man had been working on purely theoretical grounds the whole time; when he said it was "the most important" research the world had ever seen, he simply meant it squared up so many theories, settled so much that was in doubt; he had troubled no more about the application of the stuff he was going to turn out than if he had been a machine that makes guns. This was a possible substance, and he was going to make it! *V'la tout*, as the Frenchman says.

Beyond that, he was childish; if he made it, it would go down to posterity as Cavorite or Cavorine, and he would be made an FRS, and his portrait given away as a scientific worthy with *Nature*, and things like that. And that was all he saw! He would have dropped this bombshell into the world as though he had discovered a new species of gnat, if it had not happened that I had come along. And there it would have lain and fizzled, like one or two other little things these scientific people have lit and dropped about us.

When I realised this, it was I did the talking, and Cavor who said, "Go on!" I jumped up. I paced the room, gesticulating like a boy of twenty. I tried to make him understand his duties and responsibilities in the matter – *our* duties and responsibilities in the matter. I assured him we might make wealth enough to work any sort of social revolution we fancied, we might own and order the whole world. I told him of companies and patents, and the case for secret processes. All these things seemed to take him much as his mathematics had taken me. A look of perplexity came into his ruddy little face. He stammered something about indifference to wealth, but I brushed all that aside. He had got to be rich, and it was no good his stammering. I gave him to understand the sort of man I was, and that I had had very considerable business experience. I did not tell him I was an undischarged bankrupt at the time, because that was temporary, but I think I reconciled my evident poverty with my financial claims. And quite insensibly, in the way such projects grow, the understanding of a Cavorite monopoly grew up between us. He was to make the stuff, and I was to make the boom.

I stuck like a leech to the "we" – "you" and "I" didn't exist for me.

His idea was that the profits I spoke of might go to endow research, but that, of course, was a matter we had to settle later. "That's all right," I shouted, "that's all right." The great point, as I insisted, was to get the thing done.

"Here is a substance," I cried, "no home, no factory, no fortress, no ship can dare to be without – more universally applicable even than a patent medicine. There isn't a solitary aspect of it, not one of its ten thousand possible uses that will not make us rich, Cavor, beyond the dreams of avarice!"

"No!" he said. "I begin to see. It's extraordinary how one gets new points of view by talking over things!"

"And as it happens you have just talked to the right man!"

"I suppose no one," he said, "is absolutely *averse* to enormous wealth. Of course there is one thing – "

He paused. I stood still.

"It is just possible, you know, that we may not be able to make it after all! It may be one of those things that are a theoretical possibility, but a practical absurdity. Or when we make it, there may be some little hitch – !"

"We'll tackle the hitch when it comes," said I.

# CHAPTER TWO

## The First Making of Cavorite

B ut Cavor's fears were groundless, so far as the actual making was concerned. On the 14th of October, 1899, this incredible substance was made!

Oddly enough, it was made at last by accident, when Mr Cavor least expected it. He had fused together a number of metals and certain other things – I wish I knew the particulars now! – and he intended to leave the mixture a week and then allow it to cool slowly. Unless he had miscalculated, the last stage in the combination would occur when the stuff sank to a temperature of 60° Fahr. But it chanced that, unknown to Cavor, dissension had arisen about the furnace tending. Gibbs, who had previously seen to this, had suddenly attempted to shift it to the man who had been a gardener, on the score that coal was soil, being dug, and therefore could not possibly fall within the province of a joiner; the man who had been a jobbing gardener alleged, however, that coal was a metallic or ore-like substance, let alone that he was cook. But Spargus insisted on Gibbs doing the coaling, seeing that he was a joiner and that coal is notoriously fossil wood. Consequently Gibbs ceased to replenish the furnace, and no one else did so, and Cavor was too much immersed in certain interesting problems concerning a Cavorite flying machine (neglecting the resistance of the air and one or two other points) to perceive that anything was wrong. And the premature birth of his invention took place just as he was coming across the field to my bungalow for our afternoon talk and tea.

I remember the occasion with extreme vividness. The water was boiling, and everything was prepared, and the sound of his "zuzzoo" had brought me out upon the verandah. His active little figure was black against the autumnal sunset, and to the right the chimneys of his house just rose above a gloriously tinted group of trees. Remoter rose the Wealden Hills, faint and blue, while to the left the hazy marsh spread out spacious and serene. And then –

The chimneys jerked heavenward, smashing into a string of bricks as they rose, and the roof and a miscellany of furniture followed. Then overtaking them came a huge white flame. The trees about the building swayed and whirled and tore themselves to pieces, that sprang towards the flare. My ears were smitten with a clap of thunder that left me deaf on one side for life, and all about me windows smashed, unheeded.

I took three steps from the verandah towards Cavor's house, and even as I did so came the wind.

Instantly my coat-tails were over my head, and I was progressing in great leaps and bounds, and quite against my will, towards him. In the same moment the discoverer was seized, whirled about, and flew through the screaming air. I saw one of my chimney pots hit the ground within six yards of me, leap a score of feet, and so hurry in great strides towards the focus of the disturbance. Cavor, kicking and flapping, came down again, rolled over and over on the ground for a space, struggled up and was lifted and borne forward at an enormous velocity, vanishing at last among the labouring, lashing trees that writhed about his house.

A mass of smoke and ashes, and a square of bluish shining substance rushed up towards the zenith. A large fragment of fencing came sailing past me, dropped edgeways, hit the ground and fell flat, and then the worst was over. The aerial commotion fell swiftly until it was a mere strong gale, and I became once more aware that I had breath and feet. By leaning back against the wind I managed to stop, and could collect such wits as still remained to me.

In that instant the whole face of the world had changed. The tranquil sunset had vanished, the sky was dark with scurrying clouds, everything was flattened and swaying with the gale. I glanced back to see if my bungalow was still in a general way standing, then staggered forwards towards the trees amongst which Cavor had vanished, and through whose tall and leaf-denuded branches shone the flames of his burning house.

I entered the copse, dashing from one tree to another and clinging to them, and for a space I sought him in vain. Then amidst a heap of smashed branches and fencing that had banked itself against a portion of his garden wall I perceived something stir. I made a run for this, but before I reached it a brown object separated itself, rose on two muddy legs, and protruded two drooping, bleeding hands. Some tattered ends of garment fluttered out from its middle portion and streamed before the wind.

For a moment I did not recognise this earthy lump, and then I saw that it was Cavor, caked in the mud in which he had rolled.

He leant forward against the wind, rubbing the dirt from his eyes and mouth.

He extended a muddy lump of hand, and staggered a pace towards me. His face worked with emotion, little lumps of mud kept falling from it. He looked as damaged and pitiful as any living creature I have ever seen, and his remark therefore amazed me exceeding. "Gratulate me," he gasped; "gratulate me!"

"Congratulate you!" said I. "Good heavens! What for?"

"I've done it."

"You *have*. What on earth caused that explosion?"

A gust of wind blew his words away. I understood him to say that it wasn't an explosion at all. The wind hurled me into collision with him, and we stood clinging to one another.

"Try and get back to my bungalow," I bawled in his ear. He did not hear me, and shouted something about "three martyrs – science," and also something about "not much good." At the time he laboured under the impression that his three attendants had perished in the whirlwind. Happily this was incorrect. Directly he had left for my bungalow they had gone off to the public-house in Lympne to discuss the question of the furnaces over some trivial refreshment.

I repeated my suggestion of getting back to my bungalow, and this time he understood. We clung arm-in-arm and started, and managed at last to reach the shelter of as much roof as was left to me. For a space we sat in arm-chairs and panted. All the windows were broken, and the lighter articles of furniture were in great disorder, but no irrevocable damage was done. Happily the kitchen door had stood the pressure upon it, so that all my crockery and cooking materials had survived. The oil stove was still burning, and I put on the water to boil again for tea. And that prepared, I could turn on Cavor for his explanation.

"Quite correct," he insisted; "quite correct. I've done it, and it's all right."

"But," I protested. "All right! Why, there can't be a rick standing, or a fence or a thatched roof undamaged for twenty miles round..."

"It's all right – *really*. I didn't, of course, foresee this little upset. My mind was preoccupied with another problem, and I'm apt to disregard these practical side issues. But it's all right – "

"My dear sir," I cried, "don't you see you've done thousands of pounds' worth of damage?"

"There, I throw myself on your discretion. I'm not a practical man, of course, but don't you think they will regard it as a cyclone?"

"But the explosion – "

"It was not an explosion. It's perfectly simple. Only, as I say, I'm apt to overlook these little things. It's that zuzzoo business on a larger scale. Inadvertently I made this substance of mine, this Cavorite, in a thin, wide sheet..."

He paused. "You are quite clear that the stuff is opaque to gravitation, that it cuts off things from gravitating towards each other?"

"Yes," said I. "Yes."

"Well, so soon as it reached a temperature of 60° Fahr, and the process of its manufacture was complete, the air above it, the portions of roof and ceiling and floor above it ceased to have weight. I suppose you know – everybody knows nowadays – that, as a usual thing, the air *has* weight, that it presses on everything

25

at the surface of the earth, presses in all directions, with a pressure of fourteen and a half pounds to the square inch?"

"I know that," said I. "Go on."

"I know that too," he remarked. "Only this shows you how useless knowledge is unless you apply it. You see, over our Cavorite this ceased to be the case, the air there ceased to exert any pressure, and the air round it and not over the Cavorite was exerting a pressure of fourteen pounds and a half to the square inch upon this suddenly weightless air. Ah! you begin to see! The air all about the Cavorite crushed in upon the air above it with irresistible force. The air above the Cavorite was forced upward violently, the air that rushed in to replace it immediately lost weight, ceased to exert any pressure, followed suit, blew the ceiling through and the roof off...

"You perceive," he said, "it formed a sort of atmospheric fountain, a kind of chimney in the atmosphere. And if the Cavorite itself hadn't been loose and so got sucked up the chimney, does it occur to you what would have happened?"

I thought. "I suppose," I said, "the air would be rushing up and up over that infernal piece of stuff now."

"Precisely," he said. "A huge fountain – "

"Spouting into space! Good heavens! Why, it would have squirted all the atmosphere of the earth away! It would have robbed the world of air! It would have been the death of all mankind! That little lump of stuff!"

"Not exactly into space," said Cavor, "but as bad – practically. It would have whipped the air off the world as one peels a banana, and flung it thousands of miles. It would have dropped back again, of course – but on an asphyxiated world! From our point of view very little better than if it never came back!"

I stared. As yet I was too amazed to realise how all my expectations had been upset. "What do you mean to do now?" I asked.

"In the first place, if I may borrow a garden trowel I will remove some of this earth with which I am encased, and then if I may avail myself of your domestic conveniences I will have a bath. This done, we will converse more at leisure. It will be wise, I think" – he laid a muddy hand on my arm – "if nothing were said of this affair beyond ourselves. I know I have caused great damage – probably even dwelling-houses may be ruined here and there upon the countryside. But on the other hand, I cannot possibly pay for the damage I have done, and if the real cause of this is published, it will lead only to heartburning and the obstruction of my work. One cannot foresee *everything*, you know, and I cannot consent for one moment to add the burthen of practical considerations to my theorising. Later on, when you have come in with your practical mind, and Cavorite is floated – floated *is* the word, isn't it? – and it has realised all you anticipate for it, we may set matters right with these persons. But not now – not now. If no other explanation is offered, people, in the present unsatisfactory state of meteorological science, will ascribe all this to a cyclone; there might be a public subscription, and as my house has collapsed and been burnt, I should in that case receive a considerable share in the compensation, which would be extremely helpful to the prosecution of our researches. But if it is known that *I* caused this, there will be no public subscription, and everybody will be put out. Practically I should never get a chance of working in peace again. My three assistants may or may not have perished. That is a detail. If they have, it is no great loss; they were more zealous than able, and this premature event must be largely due to their joint neglect of the furnace. If they have not perished, I doubt if they have the intelligence to explain the affair. They will accept the cyclone story. And if, during the temporary unfitness of my house for occupation, I may lodge in one of the untenanted rooms of this bungalow of yours – "

He paused and regarded me.

A man of such possibilities, I reflected, is no ordinary guest to entertain.

"Perhaps," said I, rising to my feet, "we had better begin by looking for a trowel," and I led the way to the scattered vestiges of the greenhouse.

And while he was having his bath I considered the entire question alone. It was clear there were drawbacks to Mr Cavor's society I had not foreseen. The absentmindedness that had just escaped depopulating the terrestrial globe, might at any moment result in some other grave inconvenience. On the other hand I was young, my affairs were in a mess, and I was in just the mood for reckless adventure – with a chance of something good at the end of it. I had quite settled in my mind that I was to have half at least in that aspect of the affair. Fortunately I held my bungalow, as I have already explained, on a three-year agreement, without being responsible for repairs; and my furniture, such as there was of it, had been hastily purchased, was unpaid for, insured, and altogether devoid of associations. In the end I decided to keep on with him, and see the business through.

Certainly the aspect of things had changed very greatly. I no longer doubted at all the enormous possibilities of the substance, but I began to have doubts about the gun-carriage and the patent boots.

We set to work at once to reconstruct his laboratory and proceed with our experiments. Cavor talked more on my level than he had ever done before, when it came to the question of how we should make the stuff next.

"Of course we must make it again," he said, with a sort of glee I had not expected in him, "of course we must make it again. We have caught a Tartar, perhaps, but we have left the theoretical behind us for good and all. If we can possibly avoid wrecking this little planet of ours, we will. But – there *must* be risks! There must be. In experimental work there always are. And here, as a practical man, *you* must come in. For my own part it seems to me we might make it edgeways, perhaps, and very thin. Yet I don't know. I have a certain dim perception of another method. I can hardly explain it yet. But curiously enough it came into my mind, while I was rolling over and over in the mud before the wind, and very doubtful how I the whole adventure was to end, as being absolutely the thing I ought to have done."

Even with my aid we found some little difficulty, and meanwhile we kept at work restoring the laboratory. There was plenty to do before it became absolutely necessary to decide upon the precise form and method of our second attempt. Our only hitch was the strike of the three labourers, who objected to my activity as a foreman. But that matter we compromised after two days' delay.

## CHAPTER THREE

### The Building of the Sphere

I remember the occasion very distinctly when Cavor told me of his idea of the sphere. He had had intimations of it before, but at the time it seemed to come to him in a rush. We were returning to the bungalow for tea, and on the way he fell humming. Suddenly he shouted, "That's it! That finishes it! A sort of roller blind!"

"Finishes what?" I asked.

"Space – anywhere! The moon."

"What do you mean?"

"Mean? Why – it must be a sphere! That's what I mean!"

I saw I was out of it, and for a time I let him talk in his own fashion. I hadn't the ghost of an idea then of his drift. But after he had taken tea he made it clear to me.

"It's like this," he said. "Last time I ran this stuff that cuts things off from gravitation into a flat tank with an overlap that held it down. And directly it had cooled and the manufacture was completed all that uproar happened, nothing above it weighed anything, the air went squirting up, the house squirted up, and if the stuff itself hadn't squirted up too, I don't know what would

31

have happened! But suppose the substance is loose, and quite free to go up?"

"It will go up at once!"

"Exactly. With no more disturbance than firing a big gun."

"But what good will that do?"

"I'm going up with it!"

I put down my teacup and stared at him.

"Imagine a sphere," he explained, "large enough to hold two people and their luggage. It will be made of steel lined with thick glass; it will contain a proper store of solidified air, concentrated food, water distilling apparatus, and so forth. And enamelled, as it were, on the outer steel – "

"Cavorite?"

"Yes."

"But how will you get inside?"

"There was a similar problem about a dumpling."

"Yes, I know. But how?"

"That's perfectly easy. An air-tight manhole is all that is needed. That, of course, will have to be a little complicated; there will have to be a valve, so that things may be thrown out, if necessary, without much loss of air."

"Like Jules Verne's thing in *A Trip to the Moon*."

But Cavor was not a reader of fiction.

"I begin to see," I said slowly. "And you could get in and screw yourself up while the Cavorite was warm, and as soon as it cooled it would become impervious to gravitation, and off you would fly – "

"At a tangent."

"You would go off in a straight line – " I stopped abruptly. "What is to prevent the thing travelling in a straight line into space for ever?" I asked. "You're not safe to get anywhere, and if you do – how will you get back?"

"I've just thought of that," said Cavor. "That's what I meant when I said the thing is finished. The inner glass sphere can be air-tight, and, except for the manhole, continuous, and the steel sphere can be made in sections, each section capable of rolling up after the fashion of a roller blind. These can easily be worked by springs, and released and checked by electricity conveyed by platinum wires fused through the glass. All that is merely a question of detail. So you see, that except for the thickness of the blind rollers, the Cavorite exterior of the sphere will consist of windows or blinds, whichever you like to call them. Well, when all these windows or blinds are shut, no light, no heat, no gravitation, no radiant energy of any sort will get at the inside of the sphere, it will fly on through space in a straight line, as you say. But open a window, imagine one of the windows open. Then at once any heavy body that chances to be in that direction will attract us – "

I sat taking it in.

"You see?" he said.

"Oh, I *see*."

"Practically we shall be able to tack about in space just as we wish. Get attracted by this and that."

"Oh, yes. *That's* clear enough. Only – "

"Well?"

"I don't quite see what we shall do it for! It's really only jumping off the world and back again."

"Surely! For example, one might go to the moon."

"And when one got there? What would you find?"

"We should see – Oh! consider the new knowledge."

"Is there air there?"

"There may be."

"It's a fine idea," I said, "but it strikes me as a large order all the same. The moon! I'd much rather try some smaller things first."

"They're out of the question, because of the air difficulty."

"Why not apply that idea of spring blinds – Cavorite blinds in strong steel cases – to lifting weights?"

"It wouldn't work," he insisted. "After all, to go into outer space is not so much worse, if at all, than a polar expedition. Men go on polar expeditions."

"Not businessmen. And besides, they get paid for polar expeditions. And if anything goes wrong there are relief parties. But this – it's just firing ourselves off the world for nothing."

"Call it prospecting."

"You'll have to call it that... One might make a book of it perhaps," I said.

"I have no doubt there will be minerals," said Cavor.

"For example?"

"Oh! sulphur, ores, gold perhaps, possibly new elements."

"Cost of carriage," I said. "You know you're *not* a practical man. The moon's a quarter of a million miles away."

"It seems to me it wouldn't cost much to cart any weight anywhere if you packed it in a Cavorite case."

I had not thought of that. "Delivered free on head of purchaser, eh?"

"It isn't as though we were confined to the moon."

"You mean – ?"

"There's Mars – clear atmosphere, novel surroundings, exhilarating sense of lightness. It might be pleasant to go there."

"Is there air on Mars?"

"Oh, yes!"

"Seems as though you might run it as a sanatorium. By the way, how far is Mars?"

"Two hundred million miles at present," said Cavor airily; "and you go close by the sun."

My imagination was picking itself up again. "After all," I said, "there's something in these things. There's travel – "

An extraordinary possibility came rushing into my mind. Suddenly I saw, as in a vision, the whole solar system threaded with Cavorite liners and spheres *de luxe*. "Rights of pre-emption," came floating into my head – planetary rights of pre-emption. I recalled the old Spanish monopoly in American gold. It wasn't as though it was just this planet or that – it was all of them. I stared at Cavor's rubicund face, and suddenly my imagination was leaping and dancing. I stood up, I walked up and down; my tongue was unloosened.

"I'm beginning to take it in," I said; "I'm beginning to take it in." The transition from doubt to enthusiasm seemed to take scarcely any time at all. "But this is tremendous!" I cried. "This is Imperial! I haven't been dreaming of this sort of thing."

Once the chill of my opposition was removed, his own pent-up excitement had play. He too got up and paced. He too gesticulated and shouted. We behaved like men inspired. We *were* men inspired.

"We'll settle all that!" he said in answer to some incidental difficulty that had pulled me up. "We'll soon settle that! We'll start the drawings for mouldings this very night."

"We'll start them now," I responded, and we hurried off to the laboratory to begin upon this work forthwith.

I was like a child in Wonderland all that night. The dawn found us both still at work – we kept our electric light going heedless of the day. I remember now exactly how these drawings looked. I shaded and tinted while Cavor drew – smudged and haste-marked they were in every line, but wonderfully correct. We got out the orders for the steel blinds and frames we needed from that night's work, and the glass sphere was designed within a week. We gave up our afternoon conversations and our old routine altogether. We worked, and we slept and ate when we could work no longer for hunger and fatigue. Our enthusiasm infected even our three men, though they had no idea what the sphere was for. Through those days the man Gibbs gave up walking, and went everywhere, even across the room, at a sort of fussy run.

And it grew – the sphere. December passed, January – I spent a day with a broom sweeping a path through the snow from bungalow to laboratory – February, March. By the end of March the completion was in sight. In January had come a team of horses, a huge packing-case; we had our thick glass sphere now ready, and in position under the crane we had rigged to sling it into the steel shell. All the bars and blinds of the steel shell – it was not really a spherical shell, but polyhedral, with a roller blind to each facet – had arrived by February, and the lower half was bolted together. The Cavorite was half made by March, the metallic paste had gone through two of the stages in its manufacture, and we had plastered quite half of it on to the steel bars and blinds. It was astonishing how closely we kept to the lines of Cavor's first inspiration in working out the scheme. When the bolting together of the sphere was finished, he proposed to remove the rough roof of the temporary laboratory in which the work was done, and build a furnace about it. So the last stage of Cavorite making, in which the paste is heated to a dull red glow in a stream of helium, would be accomplished when it was already on the sphere.

And then we had to discuss and decide what provisions we were to take – compressed foods, concentrated essences, steel cylinders containing reserve oxygen, an arrangement for removing carbonic acid and waste from the air and restoring oxygen by means of sodium peroxide, water condensers, and so forth. I remember the little heap they made in the corner – tins, and rolls, and boxes – convincingly matter-of-fact.

It was a strenuous time, with little chance of thinking. But one day, when we were drawing near the end, an odd mood came over me. I had been bricking up the furnace all the morning, and I sat down by these possessions dead beat. Everything seemed dull and incredible.

"But look here, Cavor," I said. "After all! What's it all for?"

He smiled. "The thing now is to go."

"The moon," I reflected. "But what do you expect? I thought the moon was a dead world."

He shrugged his shoulders.

"We're going to see."

"*Are* we?" I said, and stared before me.

"You are tired," he remarked. "You'd better take a walk this afternoon."

"No," I said obstinately; "I'm going to finish this brickwork."

And I did, and insured myself a night of insomnia.

I don't think I have ever had such a night. I had some bad times before my business collapse, but the very worst of those was sweet slumber compared to this infinity of aching wakefulness. I was suddenly in the most enormous funk at the thing we were going to do.

I do not remember before that night thinking at all of the risks we were running. Now they came like that array of spectres that

37

once beleaguered Prague, and camped around me. The strangeness of what we were about to do, the unearthliness of it, overwhelmed me. I was like a man awakened out of pleasant dreams to the most horrible surroundings. I lay, eyes wide open, and the sphere seemed to get more flimsy and feeble, and Cavor more unreal and fantastic, and the whole enterprise madder and madder every moment.

I got out of bed and wandered about. I sat at the window and stared at the immensity of space. Between the stars was the void, the unfathomable darkness! I tried to recall the fragmentary knowledge of astronomy I had gained in my irregular reading, but it was all too vague to furnish any idea of the things we might expect. At last I got back to bed and snatched some moments of sleep – moments of nightmare rather – in which I fell and fell and fell for evermore into the abyss of the sky.

I astonished Cavor at breakfast. I told him shortly, "I'm not coming with you in the sphere."

I met all his protests with a sullen persistence. "The thing's too mad," I said, "and I won't come. The thing's too mad."

I would not go with him to the laboratory. I fretted about my bungalow for a time, and then took hat and stick and set out alone, I knew not whither. It chanced to be a glorious morning: a warm wind and deep blue sky, the first green of spring abroad, and multitudes of birds singing. I lunched on beef and beer in a little public-house near Elham, and startled the landlord by remarking apropos of the weather, "A man who leaves the world when days of this sort are about is a fool!"

"That's what I says when I heerd on it!" said the landlord, and I found that for one poor soul at least this world had proved excessive, and there had been a throat-cutting. I went on with a new twist to my thoughts.

In the afternoon I had a pleasant sleep in a sunny place, and went on my way refreshed. I came to a comfortable-looking inn near Canterbury. It was bright with creepers, and the landlady was a clean old woman and took my eye. I found I had just enough money to pay for my lodging with her. I decided to stop the night there. She was a talkative body, and among many other particulars I learnt she had never been to London. "Canterbury's as far as ever I been," she said. "I'm not one of your gad-about sort."

"How would you like a trip to the moon?" I cried.

"I never did hold with them ballooneys," she said, evidently under the impression that this was a common excursion enough. "I wouldn't go up in one – not for ever so."

This struck me as being funny. After I had supped I sat on a bench by the door of the inn and gossiped with two labourers about brickmaking, and motor cars, and the cricket of last year. And in the sky a faint new crescent, blue and vague as a distant Alp, sank westward over the sun.

The next day I returned to Cavor. "I am coming," I said. "I've been a little out of order, that's all."

That was the only time I felt any serious doubt of our enterprise. Nerves purely! Alter that I worked a little more carefully, and took a trudge for an hour every day. And at last, save for the heating in the furnace, our labours were at an end.

## Chapter Four

### Inside the Sphere

"**G**o on," said Cavor, as I sat across the edge of the manhole, and looked down into the black interior of the sphere. We two were alone. It was evening, the sun had set, and the stillness of the twilight was upon everything.

I drew my other leg inside and slid down the smooth glass to the bottom of the sphere, then turned to take the cans of food and other impedimenta from Cavor. The interior was warm, the thermometer stood at eighty, and as we should lose little or none of this by radiation, we were dressed in shoes and thin flannels. We had, however, a bundle of thick woollen clothing and several thick blankets to guard against mischance. By Cavor's direction I placed the packages, the cylinders of oxygen, and so forth, loosely about my feet, and soon we had everything in. He walked about the roofless shed for a time seeking anything we had overlooked, and then crawled in after me. I noted something in his hand.

"What have you got there?" I asked.

"Haven't you brought anything to read?"

"Good Lord! No."

"I forgot to tell you. There are uncertainties – The voyage may last – We may be weeks!"

"But – "

"We shall be floating in this sphere with absolutely no occupation."

"I wish I'd known – "

He peered out of the manhole. "Look!" he said. "There's something there!"

"Is there time?"

"We shall be an hour."

I looked out. It was an old number of *Tit-Bits* that one of the men must have brought. Farther away in the corner I saw a torn *Lloyd's News*. I scrambled back into the sphere with these things. "What have you got?" I said.

I took the book from his hand and read, *The Works of William Shakespeare*.

He coloured slightly. "My education has been so purely scientific – " he said apologetically.

"Never read him?"

"Never."

"He knew a little, you know – in an irregular sort of way."

"Precisely what I am told," said Cavor.

I assisted him to screw in the glass cover of the manhole, and then he pressed a stud to close the corresponding blind in the outer case. The little oblong of twilight vanished. We were in darkness.

For a time neither of us spoke. Although our case would not be impervious to sound, everything was very still. I perceived there was nothing to grip when the shock of our start should come, and I realised that I should be uncomfortable for want of a chair.

"Why have we no chairs?" I asked.

"I've settled all that," said Cavor. "We won't need them."

"Why not?"

"You will see," he said, in the tone of a man who refuses to talk.

I became silent. Suddenly it had come to me clear and vivid that I was a fool to be inside that sphere. Even now, I asked myself, is it too late to withdraw? The world outside the sphere, I knew, would be cold and inhospitable enough for me – for weeks I had been living on subsidies from Cavor – but after all, would it be as cold as the infinite zero, as inhospitable as empty space? If it had not been for the appearance of cowardice, I believe that even then I should have made him let me out. But I hesitated on that score, and hesitated, and grew fretful and angry, and the time passed.

There came a little jerk, a noise like champagne being uncorked in another room, and a faint whistling sound. For just one instant I had a sense of enormous tension, a transient conviction that my feet were pressing downward with a force of countless tons. It lasted for an infinitesimal time.

But it stirred me to action. "Cavor!" I said into the darkness, "my nerve's in rags... I don't think – "

I stopped. He made no answer.

"Confound it!" I cried; "I'm a fool! What business have I here? I'm not coming, Cavor. The thing's too risky. I'm getting out."

"You can't," he said.

"Can't! We'll soon see about that!"

43

He made no answer for ten seconds. "It's too late for us to quarrel now, Bedford," he said. "That little jerk was the start. Already we are flying as swiftly as a bullet up into the gulf of space."

"I – " I said, and then it didn't seem to matter what happened. For a time I was, as it were, stunned; I had nothing to say. It was just as if I had never heard of this idea of leaving the world before. Then I perceived an unaccountable change in my bodily sensations. It was a feeling of lightness, of unreality. Coupled with that was a queer sensation in the head, an apoplectic effect almost, and a thumping of blood-vessels at the ears. Neither of these feelings diminished as time went on, but at last I got so used to them that I experienced no inconvenience.

I heard a click, and a little glow lamp came into being.

I saw Cavor's face, as white as I felt my own to be. We regarded one another in silence. The transparent blackness of the glass behind him made him seem as though he floated in a void.

"Well, we're committed," I said at last.

"Yes," he said, "we're committed."

"Don't move," he exclaimed, at some suggestion of a gesture. "Let your muscles keep quite lax – as if you were in bed. We are in a little universe of our own. Look at those things!"

He pointed to the loose cases and bundles that had been lying on the blankets in the bottom of the sphere. I was astonished to see that they were floating now nearly a foot from the spherical wall. Then I saw from his shadow that Cavor was no longer leaning against the glass. I thrust out my hand behind me, and found that I too was suspended in space, clear of the glass.

I did not cry out nor gesticulate, but fear came upon me. It was like being held and lifted by something – you know not what.

44

The mere touch of my hand against the glass moved me rapidly. I understood what had happened, but that did not prevent my being afraid. We were cut off from all exterior gravitation, only the attraction of objects within our sphere had effect. Consequently everything that was not fixed to the glass was falling – slowly because of the slightness of our masses – towards the centre of gravity of our little world, which seemed to be somewhere about the middle of the sphere, but rather nearer to myself than Cavor, on account of my greater weight.

"We must turn round," said Cavor, "and float back to back, with the things between us."

It was the strangest sensation conceivable, floating thus loosely in space, at first indeed horribly strange, and when the horror passed, not disagreeable at all, exceeding restful; indeed, the nearest thing in earthly experience to it that I know is lying on a very thick, soft feather bed. But the quality of utter detachment and independence! I had not reckoned on things like this. I had expected a violent jerk at starting, a giddy sense of speed. Instead I felt – as if I were disembodied. It was not like the beginning of a journey; it was like the beginning of a dream.

# CHAPTER FIVE

## The Journey to the Moon

P resently Cavor extinguished the light. He said we had not overmuch energy stored, and that what we had we must economise for reading. For a time, whether it was long or short I do not know, there was nothing but blank darkness.

A question floated up out of the void. "How are we pointing?" I said. "What is our direction?"

"We are flying away from the earth at a tangent, and as the moon is near her third quarter we are going somewhere towards her. I will open a blind – "

Came a click, and then a window in the outer case yawned open. The sky outside was as black as the darkness within the sphere, but the shape of the open window was marked by an infinite number of stars.

Those who have only seen the starry sky from the earth cannot imagine its appearance when the vague, half-luminous veil of our air has been withdrawn. The stars we see on earth are the mere scattered survivors that penetrate our misty atmosphere. But now at last I could realise the meaning of the hosts of heaven!

Stranger things we were presently to see, but that airless, star-dusted sky! Of all things, I think that will be one of the last I shall forget.

The little window vanished with a click, another beside it snapped open and instantly closed, and then a third, and for a moment I had to close my eyes because of the blinding splendour of the waning moon.

For a space I had to stare at Cavor and the white-lit things about me to season my eyes to light again, before I could turn them towards that pallid glare.

Four windows were open in order that the gravitation of the moon might act upon all the substances in our sphere. I found I was no longer floating freely in space, but that my feet were resting on the glass in the direction of the moon. The blankets and cases of provisions were also creeping slowly down the glass, and presently came to rest so as to block out a portion of the view. It seemed to me, of course, that I looked "down" when I looked at the moon. On earth "down" means earthward, the way things fall, and "up" the reverse direction. Now the pull of gravitation was towards the moon, and for all I knew to the contrary our earth was overhead. And, of course, when all the Cavorite blinds were closed, "down" was towards the centre of our sphere, and "up" towards its outer wall.

It was curiously unlike earthly experience, too, to have the light coming *up* to one. On earth light falls from above, or comes slanting down sideways, but here it came from beneath our feet, and to see our shadows we had to look up.

At first it gave me a sort of vertigo to stand only on thick glass and look down upon the moon through hundreds of thousands of miles of vacant space; but this sickness passed very speedily. And then – the splendour of the sight!

The reader may imagine it best if he will lie on the ground some warm summer's night and look between his upraised feet at the moon, but for some reason, probably because the absence of air made it so much more luminous, the moon seemed already considerably larger than it does from earth. The minutest details of its surface were acutely clear. And since we did not see it through air, its outline was bright and sharp, there was no glow or halo about it, and the star-dust that covered the sky came right to its very margin, and marked the outline of its unilluminated part. And as I stood and stared at the moon between my feet, that perception of the impossible that had been with me off and on ever since our start, returned again with tenfold conviction.

"Cavor," I said, "this takes me queerly. Those companies we were going to run, and all that about minerals?"

"Well?"

"I don't see 'em here."

"No," said Cavor; "but you'll get over all that."

"I suppose I'm made to turn right side up again. Still, *this* – For a moment I could half believe there never was a world."

"That copy of *Lloyd's News* might help you."

I stared at the paper for a moment, then held it above the level of my face, and found I could read it quite easily. I struck a column of mean little advertisements. "A gentleman of private means is willing to lend money," I read. I knew that gentleman. Then somebody eccentric wanted to sell a Cutaway bicycle, "quite new and cost 15 pounds," for five pounds; and a lady in distress wished to dispose of some fish knives and forks, "a wedding present," at a great sacrifice. No doubt some simple soul was sagely examining these knives and forks, and another triumphantly riding off on that bicycle, and a third trustfully consulting that benevolent gentleman of means even as I read. I laughed, and let the paper drift from my hand.

"Are we visible from the earth?" I asked.

"Why?"

"I knew someone who was rather interested in astronomy. It occurred to me that it would be rather odd if – my friend – chanced to be looking through some telescope."

"It would need the most powerful telescope on earth even now to see us as the minutest speck."

For a time I stared in silence at the moon.

"It's a world," I said; "one feels that infinitely more than one ever did on earth. People perhaps – "

"People!" he exclaimed. "*No!* Banish all that! Think yourself a sort of ultra-arctic voyager exploring the desolate places of space. Look at it!"

He waved his hand at the shining whiteness below. "It's dead – dead! Vast extinct volcanoes, lava wildernesses, tumbled wastes of snow, or frozen carbonic acid, or frozen air, and everywhere landslip seams and cracks and gulfs. Nothing happens. Men have watched this planet systematically with telescopes for over two hundred years. How much change do you think they have seen?"

"None."

"They have traced two indisputable landslips, a doubtful crack, and one slight periodic change of colour, and that's all."

"I didn't know they'd traced even that."

"Oh, yes. But as for people!"

"By the way," I asked, "how small a thing will the biggest telescopes show upon the moon?"

"One could see a fair-sized church. One could certainly see any towns or buildings, or anything like the handiwork of men. There might perhaps be insects, something in the way of ants, for example, so that they could hide in deep burrows from the lunar light, or some new sort of creatures having no earthly parallel. That is the most probable thing, if we are to find life there at all. Think of the difference in conditions! Life must fit itself to a day as long as fourteen earthly days, a cloudless sun-blaze of fourteen days, and then a night of equal length, growing ever colder and colder under these, cold, sharp stars. In that night there must be cold, the ultimate cold, absolute zero, 273° C. below the earthly freezing point. Whatever life there is must hibernate through *that*, and rise again each day."

He mused. "One can imagine something worm-like," he said, "taking its air solid as an earth-worm swallows earth, or thick-skinned monsters – "

"By the bye," I said, "why didn't we bring a gun?"

He did not answer that question. "No," he concluded, "we just have to go. We shall see when we get there."

I remembered something. "Of course, there's my minerals, anyhow," I said; "whatever the conditions may be."

Presently he told me he wished to alter our course a little by letting the earth tug at us for a moment. He was going to open one earthward blind for thirty seconds. He warned me that it would make my head swim, and advised me to extend my hands against the glass to break my fall. I did as he directed, and thrust my feet against the bales of food cases and air cylinders to prevent their falling upon me. Then with a click the window flew open. I fell clumsily upon hands and face, and saw for a moment

51

between my black extended fingers our mother earth – a planet in a downward sky.

We were still very near – Cavor told me the distance was perhaps eight hundred miles and the huge terrestrial disc filled all heaven. But already it was plain to see that the world was a globe. The land below us was in twilight and vague, but westward the vast gray stretches of the Atlantic shone like molten silver under the receding day. I think I recognised the cloud-dimmed coast-lines of France and Spain and the south of England, and then, with a click, the shutter closed again, and I found myself in a state of extraordinary confusion sliding slowly over the smooth glass.

When at last things settled themselves in my mind again, it seemed quite beyond question that the moon was "down" and under my feet, and that the earth was somewhere away on the level of the horizon – the earth that had been "down" to me and my kindred since the beginning of things.

So slight were the exertions required of us, so easy did the practical annihilation of our weight make all we had to do, that the necessity for taking refreshment did not occur to us for nearly six hours (by Cavor's chronometer) after our start. I was amazed at that lapse of time. Even then I was satisfied with very little. Cavor examined the apparatus for absorbing carbonic acid and water, and pronounced it to be in satisfactory order, our consumption of oxygen having been extraordinarily slight. And our talk being exhausted for the time, and there being nothing further for us to do, we gave way to a curious drowsiness that had come upon us, and spreading our blankets on the bottom of the sphere in such a manner as to shut out most of the moonlight, wished each other good-night, and almost immediately fell asleep.

And so, sleeping, and sometimes talking and reading a little, and at times eating, although without any keenness of appetite,[1] but for the most part in a sort of quiescence that was neither waking nor slumber, we fell through a space of time that had neither night nor day in it, silently, softly, and swiftly down towards the moon.

---

1 It is a curious thing, that while we were in the sphere we felt not the slightest desire for food, nor did we feel the want of it when we abstained. At first we forced our appetites, but afterwards we fasted completely. Altogether we did not consume one-hundredth part of the compressed provisions we had brought with us. The amount of carbonic acid we breathed was also unnaturally low, but why this was so I am quite unable to explain.

# CHAPTER SIX

## The Landing on the Moon

I remember how one day Cavor suddenly opened six of our shutters and blinded me so that I cried aloud at him. The whole area was moon, a stupendous scimitar of white dawn with its edge hacked out by notches of darkness, the crescent shore of an ebbing tide of darkness, out of which peaks and pinnacles came glittering into the blaze of the sun. I take it the reader has seen pictures or photographs of the moon, so that I need not describe the broader features of that landscape, those spacious ringlike ranges vaster than any terrestrial mountains, their summits shining in the day, their shadows harsh and deep, the gray disordered plains, the ridges, hills, and craterlets, all passing at last from a blazing illumination into a common mystery of black. Athwart this world we were flying scarcely a hundred miles above its crests and pinnacles. And now we could see, what no eye on earth will ever see, that under the blaze of the day the harsh outlines of the rocks and ravines of the plains and crater floor grew gray and indistinct under a thickening haze, that the white of their lit surfaces broke into lumps and patches, and broke again and shrank and vanished, and that here and there strange tints of brown and olive grew and spread.

But little time we had for watching then. For now we had come to the real danger of our journey. We had to drop ever closer to the moon as we spun about it, to slacken our pace and watch our chance, until at last we could dare to drop upon its surface.

For Cavor that was a time of intense exertion; for me it was an anxious inactivity. I seemed perpetually to be getting out of his way. He leapt about the sphere from point to point with an agility that would have been impossible on earth. He was perpetually opening and closing the Cavorite windows, making calculations, consulting his chronometer by means of the glow lamp during those last eventful hours. For a long time we had all our windows closed and hung silently in darkness hurling through space.

Then he was feeling for the shutter studs, and suddenly four windows were open. I staggered and covered my eyes, drenched and scorched and blinded by the unaccustomed splendour of the sun beneath my feet. Then again the shutters snapped, leaving my brain spinning in a darkness that pressed against the eyes. And after that I floated in another vast, black silence.

Then Cavor switched on the electric light, and told me he proposed to bind all our luggage together with the blankets about it, against the concussion of our descent. We did this with our windows closed, because in that way our goods arranged themselves naturally at the centre of the sphere. That too was a strange business; we two men floating loose in that spherical space, and packing and pulling ropes. Imagine it if you can! No up nor down, and every effort resulting in unexpected movements. Now I would be pressed against the glass with the full force of Cavor's thrust, now I would be kicking helplessly in a void. Now the star of the electric light would be overhead, now under foot. Now Cavor's feet would float up before my eyes, and now we would be crossways to each other. But at last our goods were safely bound together in a big soft bale, all except two blankets with head holes that we were to wrap about ourselves.

Then for a flash Cavor opened a window moonward, and we saw that we were dropping towards a huge central crater with a number of minor craters grouped in a sort of cross about it. And then again Cavor flung our little sphere open to the scorching, blinding sun. I think he was using the sun's attraction as a brake. "Cover yourself with a blanket," he cried, thrusting himself from me, and for a moment I did not understand.

Then I hauled the blanket from beneath my feet and got it about me and over my head and eyes. Abruptly he closed the shutters again, snapped one open again and closed it, then suddenly began snapping them all open, each safely into its steel roller. There came a jar, and then we were rolling over and over, bumping against the glass and against the big bale of our luggage, and clutching at each other, and outside some white substance splashed as if we were rolling down a slope of snow...

Over, clutch, bump, clutch, bump, over...

Came a thud, and I was half buried under the bale of our possessions, and for a space everything was still. Then I could hear Cavor puffing and grunting, and the snapping of a shutter in its sash. I made an effort, thrust back our blanket-wrapped luggage, and emerged from beneath it. Our open windows were just visible as a deeper black set with stars.

We were still alive, and we were lying in the darkness of the shadow of the wall of the great crater into which we had fallen.

We sat getting our breath again, and feeling the bruises on our limbs. I don't think either of us had had a very clear expectation of such rough handling as we had received. I struggled painfully to my feet. "And now," said I, "to look at the landscape of the moon! But – ! It's tremendously dark, Cavor!"

The glass was dewy, and as I spoke I wiped at it with my blanket. "We're half an hour or so beyond the day," he said. "We must wait."

It was impossible to distinguish anything. We might have been in a sphere of steel for all that we could see. My rubbing with the blanket simply smeared the glass, and as fast as I wiped it, it became opaque again with freshly condensed moisture mixed with an increasing quantity of blanket hairs. Of course I ought not to have used the blanket. In my efforts to clear the glass I slipped upon the damp surface, and hurt my shin against one of the oxygen cylinders that protruded from our bale.

The thing was exasperating – it was absurd. Here we were just arrived upon the moon, amidst we knew not what wonders, and all we could see was the gray and streaming wall of the bubble in which we had come.

"Confound it!" I said, "but at this rate we might have stopped at home;" and I squatted on the bale and shivered, and drew my blanket closer about me.

Abruptly the moisture turned to spangles and fronds of frost. "Can you reach the electric heater," said Cavor. "Yes – that black knob. Or we shall freeze."

I did not wait to be told twice. "And now," said I, "what are we to do?"

"Wait," he said.

"Wait?"

"Of course. We shall have to wait until our air gets warm again, and then this glass will clear. We can't do anything till then. It's night here yet; we must wait for the day to overtake us. Meanwhile, don't you feel hungry?"

For a space I did not answer him, but sat fretting. I turned reluctantly from the smeared puzzle of the glass and stared at his face. "Yes," I said, "I am hungry. I feel somehow enormously disappointed. I had expected – I don't know what I had expected, but not this."

I summoned my philosophy, and rearranging my blanket about me sat down on the bale again and began my first meal on the moon. I don't think I finished it – I forget. Presently, first in patches, then running rapidly together into wider spaces, came the clearing of the glass, came the drawing of the misty veil that hid the moon world from our eyes.

We peered out upon the landscape of the moon.

# CHAPTER SEVEN

## Sunrise on the Moon

As we saw it first it was the wildest and most desolate of scenes. We were in an enormous amphitheatre, a vast circular plain, the floor of the giant crater. Its cliff-like walls closed us in on every side. From the westward the light of the unseen sun fell upon them, reaching to the very foot of the cliff, and showed a disordered escarpment of drab and grayish rock, lined here and there with banks and crevices of snow. This was perhaps a dozen miles away, but at first no intervening atmosphere diminished in the slightest the minutely detailed brilliancy with which these things glared at us. They stood out clear and dazzling against a background of starry blackness that seemed to our earthly eyes rather a gloriously spangled velvet curtain than the spaciousness of the sky.

The eastward cliff was at first merely a starless selvedge to the starry dome. No rosy flush, no creeping pallor, announced the commencing day. Only the Corona, the Zodiacal light, a huge cone-shaped, luminous haze, pointing up towards the splendour of the morning star, warned us of the imminent nearness of the sun.

Whatever light was about us was reflected by the westward cliffs. It showed a huge undulating plain, cold and gray, a gray that deepened eastward into the absolute raven darkness of the cliff shadow. Innumerable rounded gray summits, ghostly hummocks, billows of snowy substance, stretching crest beyond crest into the remote obscurity, gave us our first inkling of the distance of the crater wall. These hummocks looked like snow. At the time I thought they were snow. But they were not – they were mounds and masses of frozen air?

So it was at first, and then, sudden, swift, and amazing, came the lunar day.

The sunlight had crept down the cliff, it touched the drifted masses at its base and incontinently came striding with seven-leagued boots towards us. The distant cliff seemed to shift and quiver, and at the touch of the dawn a reek of gray vapour poured upward from the crater floor, whirls and puffs and drifting wraiths of gray, thicker and broader and denser, until at last the whole westward plain was steaming like a wet handkerchief held before the fire, and the westward cliffs were no more than a refracted glare beyond.

"It is air," said Cavor. "It must be air – or it would not rise like this – at the mere touch of a sunbeam. And at this pace..."

He peered upwards. "Look!" he said.

"What?" I asked.

"In the sky. Already. On the blackness – a little touch of blue. See! The stars seem larger. And the little ones and all those dim nebulosities we saw in empty space – they are hidden!"

Swiftly, steadily, the day approached us. Gray summit after gray summit was overtaken by the blaze, and turned to a smoking white intensity. At last there was nothing to the west of us but a bank of surging fog, the tumultuous advance and ascent of cloudy haze. The distant cliff had receded farther and farther, had loomed and changed through the whirl, and foundered and vanished at last in its confusion.

Nearer came that steaming advance, nearer and nearer, coming as fast as the shadow of a cloud before the south-west wind. About us rose a thin anticipatory haze.

Cavor gripped my arm.

"What?" I said.

"Look! The sunrise! The sun!"

He turned me about and pointed to the brow of the eastward cliff, looming above the haze about us, scarce lighter than the darkness of the sky. But now its line was marked by strange reddish shapes, tongues of vermilion flame that writhed and danced. I fancied it must be spirals of vapour that had caught the light and made this crest of fiery tongues against the sky, but indeed it was the solar prominences I saw, a crown of fire about the sun that is forever hidden from earthly eyes by our atmospheric veil.

And then – the sun!

Steadily, inevitably came a brilliant line, came a thin edge of intolerable effulgence that took a circular shape, became a bow, became a blazing sceptre, and hurled a shaft of heat at us as though it was a spear.

It seemed verily to stab my eyes! I cried aloud and turned about blinded, groping for my blanket beneath the bale.

And with that incandescence came a sound, the first sound that had reached us from without since we left the earth, a hissing and rustling, the stormy trailing of the aerial garment of the advancing day. And with the coming of the sound and the light the sphere lurched, and blinded and dazzled we staggered helplessly against each other. It lurched again, and the hissing grew louder. I had shut my eyes perforce, I was making clumsy efforts to cover my head with my blanket, and this second lurch sent me helplessly off my feet. I fell against the bale, and opening my eyes had a momentary glimpse of the air just outside our glass. It was running – it was boiling – like snow into which a white-hot rod is thrust. What had been solid air had suddenly at the touch of the sun become a paste, a mud, a slushy liquefaction, that hissed and bubbled into gas.

There came a still more violent whirl of the sphere and we had clutched one another. In another moment we were spun about again. Round we went and over, and then I was on all fours. The lunar dawn had hold of us. It meant to show us little men what the moon could do with us.

I caught a second glimpse of things without, puffs of vapour, half-liquid slush, excavated, sliding, falling, sliding. We dropped into darkness. I went down with Cavor's knees in my chest. Then he seemed to fly away from me, and for a moment I lay with all the breath out of my body staring upward. A toppling crag of the melting stuff had splashed over us, buried us, and now it thinned and boiled off us. I saw the bubbles dancing on the glass above. I heard Cavor exclaiming feebly.

Then some huge landslip in the thawing air had caught us, and spluttering expostulation, we began to roll down a slope, rolling faster and faster, leaping crevasses and rebounding from banks, faster and faster, westward into the white-hot boiling tumult of the lunar day.

Clutching at one another we spun about, pitched this way and that, our bale of packages leaping at us, pounding at us. We collided, we gripped, we were torn asunder – our heads met, and the whole universe burst into fiery darts and stars! On the earth we should have smashed one another a dozen times, but on the moon, luckily for us, our weight was only one-sixth of what it is terrestrially, and we fell very mercifully. I recall a sensation of utter sickness, a feeling as if my brain were upside down within my skull, and then –

Something was at work upon my face, some thin feelers worried my ears. Then I discovered the brilliance of the landscape around was mitigated by blue spectacles. Cavor bent over me, and I saw his face upside down, his eyes also protected by tinted goggles. His breath came irregularly, and his lip was bleeding from a bruise. "Better?" he said, wiping the blood with the back of his hand.

Everything seemed swaying for a space, but that was simply my giddiness. I perceived that he had closed some of the shutters in the outer sphere to save me from the direct blaze of the sun. I was aware that everything about us was very brilliant.

"Lord!" I gasped. "But this – !"

I craned my neck to see. I perceived there was a blinding glare outside, an utter change from the gloomy darkness of our first impressions. "Have I been insensible long?" I asked.

"I don't know – the chronometer is broken. Some little time… My dear chap! I have been afraid…"

I lay for a space taking this in. I saw his face still bore evidences of emotion. For a while I said nothing. I passed an inquisitive hand over my contusions, and surveyed his face for similar damages. The back of my right hand had suffered most, and was skinless and raw. My forehead was bruised and had bled.

He handed me a little measure with some of the restorative – I forget the name of it – he had brought with us. After a time I felt a little better. I began to stretch my limbs carefully. Soon I could talk.

"It wouldn't have done," I said, as though there had been no interval.

"No! it *wouldn't*."

He thought, his hands hanging over his knees. He peered through the glass and then stared at me. "Good Lord!" he said. "*No!*"

"What has happened?" I asked after a pause. "Have we jumped to the tropics?"

"It was as I expected. This air has evaporated – if it is air. At any rate, it has evaporated, and the surface of the moon is showing. We are lying on a bank of earthy rock. Here and there bare soil is exposed. A queer sort of soil!"

It occurred to him that it was unnecessary to explain. He assisted me into a sitting position, and I could see with my own eyes.

# CHAPTER EIGHT

## A Lunar Morning

The harsh emphasis, the pitiless black and white of scenery had altogether disappeared. The glare of the sun had taken upon itself a faint tinge of amber; the shadows upon the cliff of the crater wall were deeply purple. To the eastward a dark bank of fog still crouched and sheltered from the sunrise, but to the westward the sky was blue and clear. I began to realise the length of my insensibility.

We were no longer in a void. An atmosphere had arisen about us. The outline of things had gained in character, had grown acute and varied; save for a shadowed space of white substance here and there, white substance that was no longer air but snow, the arctic appearance had gone altogether. Everywhere broad rusty brown spaces of bare and tumbled earth spread to the blaze of the sun. Here and there at the edge of the snowdrifts were transient little pools and eddies of water, the only things stirring in that expanse of barrenness. The sunlight inundated the upper two blinds of our sphere and turned our climate to high summer, but our feet were still in shadow, and the sphere was lying upon a drift of snow.

And scattered here and there upon the slope, and emphasised by little white threads of unthawed snow upon their shady sides, were shapes like sticks, dry twisted sticks of the same rusty hue as the rock upon which they lay. That caught one's thoughts sharply. Sticks! On a lifeless world? Then as my eye grew more accustomed to the texture of their substance, I perceived that almost all this surface had a fibrous texture, like the carpet of brown needles one finds beneath the shade of pine trees.

"Cavor!" I said.

"Yes."

"It may be a dead world now – but once – "

Something arrested my attention. I had discovered among these needles a number of little round objects. And it seemed to me that one of these had moved.

"Cavor," I whispered.

"What?"

But I did not answer at once. I stared incredulous. For an instant I could not believe my eyes. I gave an inarticulate cry. I gripped his arm. I pointed. "Look!" I cried, finding my tongue. "There! Yes! And there!"

His eyes followed my pointing finger. "Eh?" he said.

How can I describe the thing I saw? It is so petty a thing to state, and yet it seemed so wonderful, so pregnant with emotion. I have said that amidst the stick-like litter were these rounded bodies, these little oval bodies that might have passed as very small pebbles. And now first one and then another had stirred, had rolled over and cracked, and down the crack of each of them showed a minute line of yellowish green, thrusting outward to meet the hot encouragement of the newly-risen sun. For a moment that was all, and then there stirred, and burst a third!

"It is a seed," said Cavor. And then I heard him whisper very softly, "*Life!*"

"Life!" And immediately it poured upon us that our vast journey had not been made in vain, that we had come to no arid waste of minerals, but to a world that lived and moved! We watched intensely. I remember I kept rubbing the glass before me with my sleeve, jealous of the faintest suspicion of mist.

The picture was clear and vivid only in the middle of the field. All about that centre the dead fibres and seeds were magnified and distorted by the curvature of the glass. But we could see enough! One after another all down the sunlit slope these miraculous little brown bodies burst and gaped apart, like seed-pods, like the husks of fruits; opened eager mouths that drank in the heat and light pouring in a cascade from the newly-risen sun.

Every moment more of these seed coats ruptured, and even as they did so the swelling pioneers overflowed their rent-distended seed-cases, and passed into the second stage of growth. With a steady assurance, a swift deliberation, these amazing seeds thrust a rootlet downward to the earth and a queer little bundle-like bud into the air. In a little while the whole slope was dotted with minute plantlets standing at attention in the blaze of the sun.

They did not stand for long. The bundle-like buds swelled and strained and opened with a jerk, thrusting out a coronet of little sharp tips, spreading a whorl of tiny, spiky, brownish leaves, that lengthened rapidly, lengthened visibly even as we watched. The movement was slower than any animal's, swifter than any plant's I have ever seen before. How can I suggest it to you – the way that growth went on? The leaf tips grew so that they moved onward even while we looked at them. The brown seed-case shrivelled and was absorbed with an equal rapidity. Have you ever on a cold day taken a thermometer into your warm hand and watched the little thread of mercury creep up the tube? These moon plants grew like that.

In a few minutes, as it seemed, the buds of the more forward of these plants had lengthened into a stem and were even putting forth a second whorl of leaves, and all the slope that had seemed so recently a lifeless stretch of litter was now dark with the stunted olive-green herbage of bristling spikes that swayed with the vigour of their growing.

I turned about, and behold! along the upper edge of a rock to the eastward a similar fringe in a scarcely less forward condition swayed and bent, dark against the blinding glare of the sun. And beyond this fringe was the silhouette of a plant mass, branching clumsily like a cactus, and swelling visibly, swelling like a bladder that fills with air.

Then to the westward also I discovered that another such distended form was rising over the scrub. But here the light fell upon its sleek sides, and I could see that its colour was a vivid orange hue. It rose as one watched it; if one looked away from it for a minute and then back, its outline had changed; it thrust out blunt congested branches until in a little time it rose a coralline shape of many feet in height. Compared with such a growth the terrestrial puff-ball, which will sometimes swell a foot in diameter in a single night, would be a hopeless laggard. But then the puff-ball grows against a gravitational pull six times that of the moon. Beyond, out of gullies and flats that had been hidden from us, but not from the quickening sun, over reefs and banks of shining rock, a bristling beard of spiky and fleshy vegetation was straining into view, hurrying tumultuously to take advantage of the brief day in which it must flower and fruit and seed again and die. It was like a miracle, that growth. So, one must imagine, the trees and plants arose at the Creation and covered the desolation of the new-made earth.

Imagine it; Imagine that dawn! The resurrection of the frozen air, the stirring and quickening of the soil, and then this silent uprising of vegetation, this unearthly ascent of fleshiness and spikes. Conceive it all lit by a blaze that would make the intensest sunlight of earth seem watery and weak. And still around this stirring jungle, wherever there was shadow, lingered banks of bluish snow. And to have the picture of our impression complete, you must bear in mind that we saw it all through a thick bent glass, distorting it as things are distorted by a lens, acute only in the centre of the picture, and very bright there, and towards the edges magnified and unreal.

# CHAPTER NINE

## Prospecting Begins

We ceased to gaze. We turned to each other, the same thought, the same question in our eyes. For these plants to grow, there must be some air, however attenuated, air that we also should be able to breathe.

"The manhole?" I said.

"Yes!" said Cavor, "if it is air we see!"

"In a little while," I said, "these plants will be as high as we are. Suppose – suppose after all – Is it certain? How do you know that stuff is air? It may be nitrogen – it may be carbonic acid even!"

"That is easy," he said, and set about proving it. He produced a big piece of crumpled paper from the bale, lit it, and thrust it hastily through the manhole valve. I bent forward and peered down through the thick glass for its appearance outside, that little flame on whose evidence depended so much!

I saw the paper drop out and lie lightly upon the snow. The pink flame of its burning vanished. For an instant it seemed to be extinguished. And then I saw a little blue tongue upon the edge of it that trembled, and crept, and spread!

Quietly the whole sheet, save where it lay in immediate contact with the snow, charred and shrivelled and sent up a quivering thread of smoke. There was no doubt left to me; the atmosphere of the moon was either pure oxygen or air, and capable therefore – unless its tenuity was excessive – of supporting our alien life. We might emerge – and live!

I sat down with my legs on either side of the manhole and prepared to unscrew it, but Cavor stopped me. "There is first a little precaution," he said. He pointed out that although it was certainly an oxygenated atmosphere outside, it might still be so rarefied as to cause us grave injury. He reminded me of mountain sickness, and of the bleeding that often afflicts aeronauts who have ascended too swiftly, and he spent some time in the preparation of a sickly-tasting drink which he insisted on my sharing. It made me feel a little numb, but otherwise had no effect on me. Then he permitted me to begin unscrewing.

Presently the glass stopper of the manhole was so far undone that the denser air within our sphere began to escape along the thread of the screw, singing as a kettle sings before it boils. Thereupon he made me desist. It speedily became evident that the pressure outside was very much less than it was within. How much less it was we had no means of telling.

I sat grasping the stopper with both hands, ready to close it again if, in spite of our intense hope, the lunar atmosphere should after all prove too rarefied for us, and Cavor sat with a cylinder of compressed oxygen at hand to restore our pressure. We looked at one another in silence, and then at the fantastic vegetation that swayed and grew visibly and noiselessly without. And ever that shrill piping continued.

My blood-vessels began to throb in my ears, and the sound of Cavor's movements diminished. I noted how still everything had become, because of the thinning of the air.

As our air sizzled out from the screw the moisture of it condensed in little puffs.

Presently I experienced a peculiar shortness of breath that lasted indeed during the whole of the time of our exposure to the moon's exterior atmosphere, and a rather unpleasant sensation about the ears and fingernails and the back of the throat grew upon my attention, and presently passed off again.

But then came vertigo and nausea that abruptly changed the quality of my courage. I gave the lid of the manhole half a turn and made a hasty explanation to Cavor; but now he was the more sanguine. He answered me in a voice that seemed extraordinarily small and remote, because of the thinness of the air that carried the sound. He recommended a nip of brandy, and set me the example, and presently I felt better. I turned the manhole stopper back again. The throbbing in my ears grew louder, and then I remarked that the piping note of the outrush had ceased. For a time I could not be sure that it had ceased.

"Well?" said Cavor, in the ghost of a voice.

"Well?" said I.

"Shall we go on?"

I thought. "Is this all?"

"If you can stand it."

By way of answer I went on unscrewing. I lifted the circular operculum from its place and laid it carefully on the bale. A flake or so of snow whirled and vanished as that thin and unfamiliar air took possession of our sphere. I knelt, and then seated myself at the edge of the manhole, peering over it. Beneath, within a yard of my face, lay the untrodden snow of the moon.

There came a little pause. Our eyes met.

"It doesn't distress your lungs too much?" said Cavor.

"No," I said. "I can stand this."

He stretched out his hand for his blanket, thrust his head through its central hole, and wrapped it about him. He sat down on the edge of the manhole, he let his feet drop until they were within six inches of the lunar ground. He hesitated for a moment, then thrust himself forward, dropped these intervening inches, and stood upon the untrodden soil of the moon.

As he stepped forward he was refracted grotesquely by the edge of the glass. He stood for a moment looking this way and that. Then he drew himself together and leapt.

The glass distorted everything, but it seemed to me even then to be an extremely big leap. He had at one bound become remote. He seemed twenty or thirty feet off. He was standing high upon a rocky mass and gesticulating back to me. Perhaps he was shouting – but the sound did not reach me. But how the deuce had he done this? I felt like a man who has just seen a new conjuring trick.

In a puzzled state of mind I too dropped through the manhole. I stood up. Just in front of me the snowdrift had fallen away and made a sort of ditch. I made a step and jumped.

I found myself flying through the air, saw the rock on which he stood coming to meet me, clutched it and clung in a state of infinite amazement.

I gasped a painful laugh. I was tremendously confused. Cavor bent down and shouted in piping tones for me to be careful.

I had forgotten that on the moon, with only an eighth part of the earth's mass and a quarter of its diameter, my weight was barely a sixth what it was on earth. But now that fact insisted on being remembered.

"We are out of Mother Earth's leading-strings now," he said.

With a guarded effort I raised myself to the top, and moving as cautiously as a rheumatic patient, stood up beside him under the blaze of the sun. The sphere lay behind us on its dwindling snowdrift thirty feet away.

As far as the eye could see over the enormous disorder of rocks that formed the crater floor, the same bristling scrub that surrounded us was starting into life, diversified here and there by bulging masses of a cactus form, and scarlet and purple lichens that grew so fast they seemed to crawl over the rocks. The whole area of the crater seemed to me then to be one similar wilderness up to the very foot of the surrounding cliff.

This cliff was apparently bare of vegetation save at its base, and with buttresses and terraces and platforms that did not very greatly attract our attention at the time. It was many miles away from us in every direction, we seemed to be almost at the centre of the crater, and we saw it through a certain haziness that drove before the wind. For there was even a wind now in the thin air, a swift yet weak wind that chilled exceedingly but exerted little pressure. It was blowing round the crater, as it seemed, to the hot illuminated side from the foggy darkness under the sunward wall. It was difficult to look into this eastward fog; we had to peer with half-closed eyes beneath the shade of our hands, because of the fierce intensity of the motionless sun.

"It seems to be deserted," said Cavor, "absolutely desolate."

I looked about me again. I retained even then a clinging hope of some quasi-human evidence, some pinnacle of building, some house or engine, but everywhere one looked spread the tumbled rocks in peaks and crests, and the darting scrub and those bulging cacti that swelled and swelled, a flat negation as it seemed of all such hope.

"It looks as though these plants had it to themselves," I said. "I see no trace of any other creature."

"No insects – no birds, no! Not a trace, not a scrap nor particle of animal life. If there was – what would they do in the night?… No; there's just these plants alone."

I shaded my eyes with my hand. "It's like the landscape of a dream. These things are less like earthly land plants than the things one imagines among the rocks at the bottom of the sea. Look at that yonder! One might imagine it a lizard changed into a plant. And the glare!"

"This is only the fresh morning," said Cavor.

He sighed and looked about him. "This is no world for men," he said. "And yet in a way – it appeals."

He became silent for a time, then commenced his meditative humming.

I started at a gentle touch, and found a thin sheet of livid lichen lapping over my shoe. I kicked at it and it fell to powder, and each speck began to grow.

I heard Cavor exclaim sharply, and perceived that one of the fixed bayonets of the scrub had pricked him.

He hesitated, his eyes sought among the rocks about us. A sudden blaze of pink had crept up a ragged pillar of crag. It was a most extraordinary pink, a livid magenta.

"Look!" said I, turning, and behold Cavor had vanished.

For an instant I stood transfixed. Then I made a hasty step to look over the verge of the rock. But in my surprise at his disappearance I forgot once more that we were on the moon. The thrust of my foot that I made in striding would have carried me a yard on earth; on the moon it carried me six – a good five yards over the edge. For the moment the thing had something of the effect of those nightmares when one falls and falls. For while one falls sixteen feet in the first second of a fall on earth, on the moon one falls two, and with only a sixth of one's weight. I fell, or rather I jumped down, about ten yards I suppose. It seemed to take quite a long time, five or six seconds, I should think. I floated through the air and fell like a feather, knee-deep in a snow-drift in the bottom of a gully of blue-gray, white-veined rock.

I looked about me. "Cavor!" I cried; but no Cavor was visible.

"Cavor!" I cried louder, and the rocks echoed me.

I turned fiercely to the rocks and clambered to the summit of them. "Cavor!" I cried. My voice sounded like the voice of a lost lamb.

The sphere, too, was not in sight, and for a moment a horrible feeling of desolation pinched my heart.

Then I saw him. He was laughing and gesticulating to attract my attention. He was on a bare patch of rock twenty or thirty yards away. I could not hear his voice, but "jump" said his gestures. I hesitated, the distance seemed enormous. Yet I reflected that surely I must be able to clear a greater distance than Cavor.

I made a step back, gathered myself together, and leapt with all my might. I seemed to shoot right up in the air as though I should never come down.

It was horrible and delightful, and as wild as a nightmare, to go flying off in this fashion. I realised my leap had been altogether too violent. I flew clean over Cavor's head and beheld a spiky confusion in a gully spreading to meet my fall. I gave a yelp of alarm. I put out my hands and straightened my legs.

I hit a huge fungoid bulk that burst all about me, scattering a mass of orange spores in every direction, and covering me with orange powder. I rolled over spluttering, and came to rest convulsed with breathless laughter.

I became aware of Cavor's little round face peering over a bristling hedge. He shouted some faded inquiry. "Eh?" I tried to shout, but could not do so for want of breath. He made his way towards me, coming gingerly among the bushes.

"We've got to be careful," he said. "This moon has no discipline. She'll let us smash ourselves."

He helped me to my feet. "You exerted yourself too much," he said, dabbing at the yellow stuff with his hand to remove it from my garments.

I stood passive and panting, allowing him to beat off the jelly from my knees and elbows and lecture me upon my misfortunes. "We don't quite allow for the gravitation. Our muscles are scarcely educated yet. We must practise a little, when you have got your breath."

I pulled two or three little thorns out of my hand, and sat for a time on a boulder of rock. My muscles were quivering, and I had that feeling of personal disillusionment that comes at the first fall to the learner of cycling on earth.

It suddenly occurred to Cavor that the cold air in the gully, after the brightness of the sun, might give me a fever. So we clambered back into the sunlight. We found that beyond a few abrasions I had received no serious injuries from my tumble, and at Cavor's suggestion we were presently looking round for some safe and easy landing-place for my next leap. We chose a rocky slab some ten yards off, separated from us by a little thicket of olive-green spikes.

"Imagine it there!" said Cavor, who was assuming the airs of a trainer, and he pointed to a spot about four feet from my toes. This leap I managed without difficulty, and I must confess I found a certain satisfaction in Cavor's falling short by a foot or so and tasting the spikes of the scrub. "One has to be careful you see," he said, pulling out his thorns, and with that he ceased to be my Mentor and became my fellow-learner in the art of lunar locomotion.

We chose a still easier jump and did it without difficulty, and then leapt back again, and to and fro several times, accustoming our muscles to the new standard. I could never have believed had I not experienced it, how rapid that adaptation would be. In a very little time indeed, certainly after fewer than thirty leaps, we could judge the effort necessary for a distance with almost terrestrial assurance.

And all this time the lunar plants were growing around us, higher and denser and more entangled, every moment thicker and taller, spiked plants, green cactus masses, fungi, fleshy and lichenous things, strangest radiate and sinuous shapes. But we were so intent upon our leaping, that for a time we gave no heed to their unfaltering expansion.

An extraordinary elation had taken possession of us. Partly, I think, it was our sense of release from the confinement of the sphere. Mainly, however, the thin sweetness of the air, which I am certain contained a much larger proportion of oxygen than our terrestrial atmosphere. In spite of the strange quality of all about us, I felt as adventurous and experimental as a cockney would do placed for the first time among mountains and I do not think it occurred to either of us, face to face though we were with the unknown, to be very greatly afraid.

We were bitten by a spirit of enterprise. We selected a lichenous kopje perhaps fifteen yards away, and landed neatly on its summit one after the other. "Good!" we cried to each other; "good!" and Cavor made three steps and went off to a tempting slope of snow a good twenty yards and more beyond. I stood for a moment struck by the grotesque effect of his soaring figure – his dirty cricket cap, and spiky hair, his little round body, his arms and his knickerbockered legs tucked up tightly – against the weird spaciousness of the lunar scene. A gust of laughter seized me, and then I stepped off to follow. Plump! I dropped beside him.

We made a few gargantuan strides, leapt three or four times more, and sat down at last in a lichenous hollow. Our lungs were painful. We sat holding our sides and recovering our breath, looking appreciation to one another. Cavor panted something about "amazing sensations." And then came a thought into my head. For the moment it did not seem a particularly appalling thought, simply a natural question arising out of the situation.

"By the way," I said, "where exactly is the sphere?"

Cavor looked at me. "Eh?"

The full meaning of what we were saying struck me sharply.

"Cavor!" I cried, laying a hand on his arm, "where is the sphere?"

# CHAPTER TEN

## Lost Men in the Woods

His face caught something of my dismay. He stood up and stared about him at the scrub that fenced us in and rose about us, straining upward in a passion of growth. He put a dubious hand to his lips. He spoke with a sudden lack of assurance. "I think," he said slowly, "we left it...somewhere... about *there*."

He pointed a hesitating finger that wavered in an arc.

"I'm not sure." His look of consternation deepened. "Anyhow," he said, with his eyes on me, "it can't be far."

We had both stood up. We made unmeaning ejaculations, our eyes sought in the twining, thickening jungle round about us.

All about us on the sunlit slopes frothed and swayed the darting shrubs, the swelling cactus, the creeping lichens, and wherever the shade remained the snow-drifts lingered. North, south, east, and west spread an identical monotony of unfamiliar forms. And somewhere, buried already among this tangled confusion, was our sphere, our home, our only provision, our only hope of escape from this fantastic wilderness of ephemeral growths into which we had come.

"I think after all," he said, pointing suddenly, "it might be over there."

"No," I said. "We have turned in a curve. See! here is the mark of my heels. It's clear the thing must be more to the eastward, much more. No! – the sphere must be over there."

"I *think*," said Cavor, "I kept the sun upon my right all the time."

"Every leap, it seems to *me*," I said, "my shadow flew before me."

We stared into one another's eyes. The area of the crater had become enormously vast to our imaginations, the growing thickets already impenetrably dense.

"Good heavens! What fools we have been!"

"It's evident that we must find it again," said Cavor, "and that soon. The sun grows stronger. We should be fainting with the heat already if it wasn't so dry. And... I'm hungry."

I stared at him. I had not suspected this aspect of the matter before. But it came to me at once – a positive craving. "Yes," I said with emphasis. "I am hungry too."

He stood up with a look of active resolution. "Certainly we must find the sphere."

As calmly as possible we surveyed the interminable reefs and thickets that formed the floor of the crater, each of us weighing in silence the chances of our finding the sphere before we were overtaken by heat and hunger.

"It can't be fifty yards from here," said Cavor, with indecisive gestures. "The only thing is to beat round about until we come upon it."

"That is all we can do," I said, without any alacrity to begin our hunt. "I wish this confounded spike bush did not grow so fast!"

"That's just it," said Cavor. "But it *was* lying on a bank of snow."

I stared about me in the vain hope of recognising some knoll or shrub that had been near the sphere. But everywhere was a confusing sameness, everywhere the aspiring bushes, the distending fungi, the dwindling snow banks, steadily and inevitably changed. The sun scorched and stung, the faintness of an unaccountable hunger mingled with our infinite perplexity. And even as we stood there, confused and lost amidst unprecedented things, we became aware for the first time of a sound upon the moon other than the air of the growing plants, the faint sighing of the wind, or those that we ourselves had made.

Boom... Boom... Boom...

It came from beneath our feet, a sound in the earth. We seemed to hear it with our feet as much as with our ears. Its dull resonance was muffled by distance, thick with the quality of intervening substance. No sound that I can imagine could have astonished us more, or have changed more completely the quality of things about us. For this sound, rich, slow, and deliberate, seemed to us as though it could be nothing but the striking of some gigantic buried clock.

Boom... Boom... Boom...

Sound suggestive of still cloisters, of sleepless nights in crowded cities, of vigils and the awaited hour, of all that is orderly and methodical in life, booming out pregnant and mysterious in this fantastic desert! To the eye everything was unchanged: the desolation of bushes and cacti waving silently in the wind,

85

stretched unbroken to the distant cliffs, the still dark sky was empty overhead, and the hot sun hung and burned. And through it all, a warning, a threat, throbbed this enigma of sound.

Boom... Boom... Boom...

We questioned one another in faint and faded voices. "A clock?"

"Like a clock!"

"What is it?"

"What can it be?"

"Count," was Cavor's belated suggestion, and at that word the striking ceased.

The silence, the rhythmic disappointment of the silence, came as a fresh shock. For a moment one could doubt whether one had ever heard a sound. Or whether it might not still be going on. Had I indeed heard a sound?

I felt the pressure of Cavor's hand upon my arm. He spoke in an undertone, as though he feared to wake some sleeping thing. "Let us keep together," he whispered, "and look for the sphere. We must get back to the sphere. This is beyond our understanding."

"Which way shall we go?"

He hesitated. An intense persuasion of presences, of unseen things about us and near us, dominated our minds. What could they be? Where could they be? Was this arid desolation, alternately frozen and scorched, only the outer rind and mask of some subterranean world? And if so, what sort of world? What sort of inhabitants might it not presently disgorge upon us?

And then, stabbing the aching stillness as vivid and sudden as an unexpected thunderclap, came a clang and rattle as though great gates of metal had suddenly been flung apart.

It arrested our steps. We stood gaping helplessly. Then Cavor stole towards me.

"I do not understand!" he whispered close to my face. He waved his hand vaguely skyward, the vague suggestion of still vaguer thoughts.

"A hiding-place! If anything came…"

I looked about us. I nodded my head in assent to him.

We started off, moving stealthily with the most exaggerated precautions against noise. We went towards a thicket of scrub. A clangour like hammers flung about a boiler hastened our steps. "We must crawl," whispered Cavor.

The lower leaves of the bayonet plants, already overshadowed by the newer ones above, were beginning to wilt and shrivel so that we could thrust our way in among the thickening stems without serious injury. A stab in the face or arm we did not heed. At the heart of the thicket I stopped, and stared panting into Cavor's face.

"Subterranean," he whispered. "Below."

"They may come out."

"We must find the sphere!"

"Yes," I said; "but how?"

"Crawl till we come to it."

"But if we don't?"

"Keep hidden. See what they are like."

"We will keep together," said I.

He thought. "Which way shall we go?"

"We must take our chance."

We peered this way and that. Then very circumspectly, we began to crawl through the lower jungle, making, so far as we could judge, a circuit, halting now at every waving fungus, at every sound, intent only on the sphere from which we had so foolishly emerged. Ever and again from out of the earth beneath us came concussions, beatings, strange, inexplicable, mechanical sounds; and once, and then again, we thought we heard something, a faint rattle and tumult, borne to us through the air. But fearful as we were we dared essay no vantage-point to survey the crater. For long we saw nothing of the beings whose sounds were so abundant and insistent. But for the faintness of our hunger and the drying of our throats that crawling would have had the quality of a very vivid dream. It was so absolutely unreal. The only element with any touch of reality was these sounds.

Figure it to yourself! About us the dream-like jungle, with the silent bayonet leaves darting overhead, and the silent, vivid, sun-splashed lichens under our hands and knees, waving with the vigour of their growth as a carpet waves when the wind gets beneath it. Ever and again one of the bladder fungi, bulging and distending under the sun, loomed upon us. Ever and again some novel shape in vivid colour obtruded. The very cells that built up these plants were as large as my thumb, like beads of coloured glass. And all these things were saturated in the unmitigated glare of the sun, were seen against a sky that was bluish black and spangled still, in spite of the sunlight, with a few surviving stars. Strange! the very forms and texture of the stones were strange. It was all strange, the feeling of one's body was unprecedented, every other movement ended in a surprise. The breath sucked thin in one's throat, the blood flowed through one's ears in a throbbing tide – thud, thud, thud, thud…

And ever and again came gusts of turmoil, hammering, the clanging and throb of machinery, and presently – the bellowing of great beasts!

# CHAPTER ELEVEN

## The Mooncalf Pastures

So we two poor terrestrial castaways, lost in that wild-growing moon jungle, crawled in terror before the sounds that had come upon us. We crawled, as it seemed, a long time before we saw either Selenite or mooncalf, though we heard the bellowing and gruntulous noises of these latter continually drawing nearer to us. We crawled through stony ravines, over snow slopes, amidst fungi that ripped like thin bladders at our thrust, emitting a watery humour, over a perfect pavement of things like puff-balls, and beneath interminable thickets of scrub. And ever more helplessly our eyes sought for our abandoned sphere. The noise of the mooncalves would at times be a vast flat calf-like sound, at times it rose to an amazed and wrathy bellowing, and again it would become a clogged bestial sound, as though these unseen creatures had sought to eat and bellow at the same time.

Our first view was but an inadequate transitory glimpse, yet none the less disturbing because it was incomplete. Cavor was crawling in front at the time, and he first was aware of their proximity. He stopped dead, arresting me with a single gesture.

A crackling and smashing of the scrub appeared to be advancing directly upon us, and then, as we squatted close and endeavoured to judge of the nearness and direction of this noise, there came a terrific bellow behind us, so close and vehement that the tops of the bayonet scrub bent before it, and one felt the breath of it hot and moist. And, turning about, we saw indistinctly through a crowd of swaying stems the mooncalf's shining sides, and the long line of its back loomed out against the sky.

Of course it is hard for me now to say how much I saw at that time, because my impressions were corrected by subsequent observation. First of all impressions was its enormous size; the girth of its body was some fourscore feet, its length perhaps two hundred. Its sides rose and fell with its laboured breathing. I perceived that its gigantic, flabby body lay along the ground, and that its skin was of a corrugated white, dappling into blackness along the backbone. But of its feet we saw nothing. I think also that we saw then the profile at least of the almost brainless head, with its fat-encumbered neck, its slobbering omnivorous mouth, its little nostrils, and tight shut eyes. (For the mooncalf invariably shuts its eyes in the presence of the sun.) We had a glimpse of a vast red pit as it opened its mouth to bleat and bellow again; we had a breath from the pit, and then the monster heeled over like a ship, dragged forward along the ground, creasing all its leathery skin, rolled again, and so wallowed past us, smashing a path amidst the scrub, and was speedily hidden from our eyes by the dense interlacings beyond. Another appeared more distantly, and then another, and then, as though he was guiding these animated lumps of provender to their pasture, a Selenite came momentarily into ken. My grip upon

Cavor's foot became convulsive at the sight of him, and we remained motionless and peering long after he had passed out of our range.

By contrast with the mooncalves he seemed a trivial being, a mere ant, scarcely five feet high. He was wearing garments of some leathery substance, so that no portion of his actual body appeared, but of this, of course, we were entirely ignorant. He presented himself, therefore, as a compact, bristling creature, having much of the quality of a complicated insect, with whip-like tentacles and a clanging arm projecting from his shining cylindrical body case. The form of his head was hidden by his enormous many-spiked helmet – we discovered afterwards that he used the spikes for prodding refractory mooncalves – and a pair of goggles of darkened glass, set very much at the side, gave a bird-like quality to the metallic apparatus that covered his face. His arms did not project beyond his body case, and he carried himself upon short legs that, wrapped though they were in warm coverings, seemed to our terrestrial eyes inordinately flimsy. They had very short thighs, very long shanks, and little feet.

In spite of his heavy-looking clothing, he was progressing with what would be, from the terrestrial point of view, very considerable strides, and his clanging arm was busy. The quality of his motion during the instant of his passing suggested haste and a certain anger, and soon after we had lost sight of him we heard the bellow of a mooncalf change abruptly into a short, sharp squeal followed by the scuffle of its acceleration. And gradually that bellowing receded, and then came to an end, as if the pastures sought had been attained.

We listened. For a space the moon world was still. But it was some time before we resumed our crawling search for the vanished sphere.

When next we saw mooncalves they were some little distance away from us in a place of tumbled rocks. The less vertical surfaces of the rocks were thick with a speckled green plant growing in dense mossy clumps, upon which these creatures were browsing. We stopped at the edge of the reeds amidst which we were crawling at the sight of them, peering out at them and looking round for a second glimpse of a Selenite. They lay against their food like stupendous slugs, huge, greasy hulls, eating greedily and noisily, with a sort of sobbing avidity. They seemed monsters of mere fatness, clumsy and overwhelmed to a degree that would make a Smithfield ox seem a model of agility. Their busy, writhing, chewing mouths, and eyes closed, together with the appetising sound of their munching, made up an effect of animal enjoyment that was singularly stimulating to our empty frames.

"Hogs!" said Cavor, with unusual passion. "Disgusting hogs!" and after one glare of angry envy crawled off through the bushes to our right. I stayed long enough to see that the speckled plant was quite hopeless for human nourishment, then crawled after him, nibbling a quill of it between my teeth.

Presently we were arrested again by the proximity of a Selenite, and this time we were able to observe him more exactly. Now we could see that the Selenite covering was indeed clothing, and not a sort of crustacean integument. He was quite similar in his costume to the former one we had glimpsed, except that ends of something like wadding were protruding from his neck, and he stood on a promontory of rock and moved his head this way and that, as though he was surveying the crater. We lay quite still, fearing to attract his attention if we moved, and after a time he turned about and disappeared.

We came upon another drove of mooncalves bellowing up a ravine, and then we passed over a place of sounds, sounds of beating machinery as if some huge hall of industry came near the surface there. And while these sounds were still about us we came to the edge of a great open space, perhaps two hundred yards in diameter, and perfectly level. Save for a few lichens that advanced from its margin this space was bare, and presented a powdery surface of a dusty yellow colour. We were afraid to strike out across this space, but as it presented less obstruction to our crawling than the scrub, we went down upon it and began very circumspectly to skirt its edge.

For a little while the noises from below ceased and everything, save for the faint stir of the growing vegetation, was very still. Then abruptly there began an uproar, louder, more vehement, and nearer than any we had so far heard. Of a certainty it came from below. Instinctively we crouched as flat as we could, ready for a prompt plunge into the thicket beside us. Each knock and throb seemed to vibrate through our bodies. Louder grew this throbbing and beating, and that irregular vibration increased until the whole moon world seemed to be jerking and pulsing.

"Cover," whispered Cavor, and I turned towards the bushes.

At that instant came a thud like the thud of a gun, and then a thing happened – it still haunts me in my dreams. I had turned my head to look at Cavor's face, and thrust out my hand in front of me as I did so. And my hand met nothing! Plunged suddenly into a bottomless hole!

My chest hit something hard, and I found myself with my chin on the edge of an unfathomable abyss that had suddenly opened beneath me, my hand extended stiffly into the void. The whole of that flat circular area was no more than a gigantic lid, that was now sliding sideways from off the pit it had covered into a slot prepared for it.

Had it not been for Cavor I think I should have remained rigid, hanging over this margin and staring into the enormous gulf below, until at last the edges of the slot scraped me off and hurled me into its depths. But Cavor had not received the shock that had paralysed me. He had been a little distance from the edge when the lid had first opened, and perceiving the peril that held me helpless, gripped my legs and pulled me backward. I came into a sitting position, crawled away from the edge for a space on all fours, then staggered up and ran after him across the thundering, quivering sheet of metal. It seemed to be swinging open with a steadily accelerated velocity, and the bushes in front of me shifted sideways as I ran.

I was none too soon. Cavor's back vanished amidst the bristling thicket, and as I scrambled up after him, the monstrous valve came into its position with a clang. For a long time we lay panting, not daring to approach the pit.

But at last very cautiously and bit by bit we crept into a position from which we could peer down. The bushes about us creaked and waved with the force of a breeze that was blowing down the shaft. We could see nothing at first except smooth vertical walls descending at last into an impenetrable black. And then very gradually we became aware of a number of very faint and little lights going to and fro.

For a time that stupendous gulf of mystery held us so that we forgot even our sphere. In time, as we grew more accustomed to the darkness, we could make out very small, dim, elusive shapes moving about among those needle-point illuminations. We peered amazed and incredulous, understanding so little that we could find no words to say. We could distinguish nothing that would give us a clue to the meaning of the faint shapes we saw.

"What can it be?" I asked; "what can it be?"

"The engineering!... They must live in these caverns during the night, and come out during the day."

"Cavor!" I said. "Can they be – *that* – it was something like – men?"

"*That* was not a man."

"We dare risk nothing!"

"We dare do nothing until we find the sphere!"

"We can do nothing until we find the sphere."

He assented with a groan and stirred himself to move. He stared about him for a space, sighed, and indicated a direction. We struck out through the jungle. For a time we crawled resolutely, then with diminishing vigour.

Presently among great shapes of flabby purple there came a noise of trampling and cries about us. We lay close, and for a long time the sounds went to and fro and very near. But this time we saw nothing. I tried to whisper to Cavor that I could hardly go without food much longer, but my mouth had become too dry for whispering.

"Cavor," I said, "I must have food."

He turned a face full of dismay towards me. "It's a case for holding out," he said.

"But I *must*," I said, "and look at my lips!"

95

"I've been thirsty some time."

"If only some of that snow had remained!"

"It's clean gone! We're driving from arctic to tropical at the rate of a degree a minute…"

I gnawed my hand.

"The sphere!" he said. "There is nothing for it but the sphere."

We roused ourselves to another spurt of crawling. My mind ran entirely on edible things, on the hissing profundity of summer drinks, more particularly I craved for beer. I was haunted by the memory of a sixteen gallon cask that had swaggered in my Lympne cellar. I thought of the adjacent larder, and especially of steak and kidney pie – tender steak and plenty of kidney, and rich, thick gravy between. Ever and again I was seized with fits of hungry yawning. We came to flat places overgrown with fleshy red things, monstrous coralline growths; as we pushed against them they snapped and broke. I noted the quality of the broken surfaces. The confounded stuff certainly looked of a biteable texture. Then it seemed to me that it smelt rather well.

I picked up a fragment and sniffed at it.

"Cavor," I said in a hoarse undertone.

He glanced at me with his face screwed up. "Don't," he said. I put down the fragment, and we crawled on through this tempting fleshiness for a space.

"Cavor," I asked, "why *not?*"

"Poison," I heard him say, but he did not look round.

We crawled some way before I decided.

"I'll chance it," said I.

He made a belated gesture to prevent me. I stuffed my mouth full. He crouched watching my face, his own twisted into the oddest expression. "It's good," I said.

"O Lord!" he cried.

He watched me munch, his face wrinkled between desire and disapproval, then suddenly succumbed to appetite and began to tear off huge mouthfuls. For a time we did nothing but eat.

The stuff was not unlike a terrestrial mushroom, only it was much laxer in texture, and, as one swallowed it, it warmed the throat. At first we experienced a mere mechanical satisfaction in eating; then our blood began to run warmer, and we tingled at the lips and fingers, and then new and slightly irrelevant ideas came bubbling up in our minds.

"Its good," said I. "Infernally good! What a home for our surplus population! Our poor surplus population," and I broke off another large portion. It filled me with a curiously benevolent satisfaction that there was such good food in the moon. The depression of my hunger gave way to an irrational exhilaration. The dread and discomfort in which I had been living vanished entirely. I perceived the moon no longer as a planet from which I most earnestly desired the means of escape, but as a possible refuge from human destitution. I think I forgot the Selenites, the mooncalves, the lid, and the noises completely so soon as I had eaten that fungus.

Cavor replied to my third repetition of my "surplus population" remark with similar words of approval. I felt that my head swam, but I put this down to the stimulating effect of food after a long fast. "Ess'lent discov'ry yours, Cavor," said I. "Se'nd on'y to the 'tato."

"Whajer mean?" asked Cavor. " 'Scovery of the moon – se'nd on'y to the 'tato?"

I looked at him, shocked at his suddenly hoarse voice, and by the badness of his articulation. It occurred to me in a flash that he was intoxicated, possibly by the fungus. It also occurred to me that he erred in imagining that he had discovered the moon; he had not discovered it, he had only reached it. I tried to lay my hand on his arm and explain this to him, but the issue was too subtle for his brain. It was also unexpectedly difficult to express. After a momentary attempt to understand me – I remember wondering if the fungus had made my eyes as fishy as his – he set off upon some observations on his own account.

"We are," he announced with a solemn hiccup, "the creashurs o' what we eat and drink."

He repeated this, and as I was now in one of my subtle moods, I determined to dispute it. Possibly I wandered a little from the point. But Cavor certainly did not attend at all properly. He stood up as well as he could, putting a hand on my head to steady himself, which was disrespectful, and stood staring about him, quite devoid now of any fear of the moon beings.

I tried to point out that this was dangerous for some reason that was not perfectly clear to me, but the word "dangerous" had somehow got mixed with "indiscreet," and came out rather more like "injurious" than either; and after an attempt to disentangle them, I resumed my argument, addressing myself principally to the unfamiliar but attentive coralline growths on either side. I felt that it was necessary to clear up this confusion between the moon and a potato at once – I wandered into a long parenthesis on the importance of precision of definition in argument. I did my best to ignore the fact that my bodily sensations were no longer agreeable.

In some way that I have now forgotten, my mind was led back to projects of colonisation. "We must annex this moon," I said. "There must be no shilly-shally. This is part of the White Man's Burthen. Cavor – we are – *hic* – Satap – mean Satraps! Nempire Ceasar never dreamt. B'in all the newspapers. Cavorecia. Bedfordecia. Bedfordecia – hic – Limited. Mean – unlimited! Practically."

Certainly I was intoxicated.

I embarked upon an argument to show the infinite benefits our arrival would confer on the moon. I involved myself in a rather difficult proof that the arrival of Columbus was, on the whole, beneficial to America. I found I had forgotten the line of argument I had intended to pursue, and continued to repeat "Simlar to C'lumbus," to fill up time.

From that point my memory of the action of that abominable fungus becomes confused. I remember vaguely that we declared our intention of standing no nonsense from any confounded insects, that we decided it ill became men to hide shamefully upon a mere satellite, that we equipped ourselves with huge armfuls of the fungus – whether for missile purposes or not I do not know – and, heedless of the stabs of the bayonet scrub, we started forth into the sunshine.

Almost immediately we must have come upon the Selenites. There were six of them, and they were marching in single file over a rocky place, making the most remarkable piping and whining sounds. They all seemed to become aware of us at once, all instantly became silent and motionless, like animals, with their faces turned towards us.

For a moment I was sobered.

"Insects," murmured Cavor, "insects! And they think I'm going to crawl about on my stomach – on my vertebrated stomach!"

"Stomach," he repeated slowly, as though he chewed the indignity.

Then suddenly, with a shout of fury, he made three vast strides and leapt towards them. He leapt badly; he made a series of somersaults in the air, whirled right over them, and vanished with an enormous splash amidst the cactus bladders. What the Selenites made of this amazing, and to my mind undignified irruption from another planet, I have no means of guessing. I seem to remember the sight of their backs as they ran in all directions, but I am not sure. All these last incidents before oblivion came are vague and faint in my mind. I know I made a step to follow Cavor, and tripped and fell headlong among the rocks. I was, I am certain, suddenly and vehemently ill. I seem to remember, a violent struggle and being gripped by metallic clasps...

My next clear recollection is that we were prisoners at we knew not what depths beneath the moon's surface; we were in darkness amidst strange distracting noises; our bodies were covered with scratches and bruises, and our heads racked with pain.

# Chapter Twelve

## The Selenite's Face

I found myself sitting crouched together in a tumultuous darkness. For a long time I could not understand where I was, nor how I had come to this perplexity. I thought of the cupboard into which I had been thrust at times when I was a child, and then of a very dark and noisy bedroom in which I had slept during an illness. But these sounds about me were not the noises I had known, and there was a thin flavour in the air like the wind of a stable. Then I supposed we must still be at work upon the sphere, and that somehow I had got into the cellar of Cavor's house. I remembered we had finished the sphere, and fancied I must still be in it and travelling through space.

"Cavor," I said, "cannot we have some light?"

There came no answer.

"Cavor!" I insisted.

I was answered by a groan. "My head!" I heard him say; "my head!"

I attempted to press my hands to my brow, which ached, and discovered they were tied together. This startled me very much. I brought them up to my mouth and felt the cold smoothness of metal. They were chained together. I tried to separate my legs and made out they were similarly fastened, and also that I was fastened to the ground by a much thicker chain about the middle of my body.

I was more frightened than I had yet been by anything in all our strange experiences. For a time I tugged silently at my bonds. "Cavor!" I cried out sharply. "Why am I tied? Why have you tied me hand and foot?"

"I haven't tied you," he answered. "It's the Selenites."

The Selenites! My mind hung on that for a space. Then my memories came back to me: the snowy desolation, the thawing of the air, the growth of the plants, our strange hopping and crawling among the rocks and vegetation of the crater. All the distress of our frantic search for the sphere returned to me... Finally the opening of the great lid that covered the pit!

Then as I strained to trace our later movements down to our present plight, the pain in my head became intolerable. I came to an insurmountable barrier, an obstinate blank.

"Cavor!"

"Yes?"

"Where are we?"

"How should I know?"

"Are we dead?"

"What nonsense!"

"They've got us, then!"

He made no answer but a grunt. The lingering traces of the poison seemed to make him oddly irritable.

"What do you mean to do?"

"How should I know what to do?"

"Oh, very well!" said I, and became silent. Presently, I was roused from a stupor. "O *Lord!*" I cried; "I wish you'd stop that buzzing!"

We lapsed into silence again, listening to the dull confusion of noises like the muffled sounds of a street or factory that filled our ears. I could make nothing of it, my mind pursued first one rhythm and then another, and questioned it in vain. But after a long time I became aware of a new and sharper element, not mingling with the rest but standing out, as it were, against that cloudy background of sound. It was a series of relatively very little definite sounds, tappings and rubbings, like a loose spray of ivy against a window or a bird moving about upon a box. We listened and peered about us, but the darkness was a velvet pall. There followed a noise like the subtle movement of the wards of a well-oiled lock. And then there appeared before me, hanging as it seemed in an immensity of black, a thin bright line.

"Look!" whispered Cavor very softly.

"What is it?"

"I don't know."

We stared.

The thin bright line became a band, and broader and paler. It took upon itself the quality of a bluish light falling upon a whitewashed wall. It ceased to be parallel-sided; it developed a deep indentation on one side. I turned to remark this to Cavor, and was amazed to see his ear in a brilliant illumination – all the rest of him in shadow. I twisted my head round as well as my bonds would permit. "Cavor," I said, "it's behind!"

His ear vanished – gave place to an eye!

Suddenly the crack that had been admitting the light broadened out, and revealed itself as the space of an opening door. Beyond was a sapphire vista, and in the doorway stood a grotesque outline silhouetted against the glare.

We both made convulsive efforts to turn, and failing, sat staring over our shoulders at this. My first impression was of some clumsy quadruped with lowered head. Then I perceived it was the slender pinched body and short and extremely attenuated bandy legs of a Selenite, with his head depressed between his shoulders. He was without the helmet and body covering they wear upon the exterior.

He was a blank, black figure to us, but instictively our imaginations supplied features to his very human outline. I, at least, took it instantly that he was somewhat hunchbacked, with a high forehead and long features.

He came forward three steps and paused for a time. His movements seemed absolutely noiseless. Then he came forward again. He walked like a bird, his feet fell one in front of the other. He stepped out of the ray of light that came through the doorway, and it seemed as though he vanished altogether in the shadow.

For a moment my eyes sought him in the wrong place, and then I perceived him standing facing us both in the full light. Only the human features I had attributed to him were not there at all!

Of course I ought to have expected that, only I didn't. It came to me as an absolute, for a moment an overwhelming shock. It seemed as though it wasn't a face, as though it must needs be a mask, a horror, a deformity, that would presently be disavowed or explained. There was no nose, and the thing had dull bulging eyes at the side – in the silhouette I had supposed they were ears. There were no ears... I have tried to draw one of these heads, but

I cannot. There was a mouth, downwardly curved, like a human mouth in a face that stares ferociously...

The neck on which the head was poised was jointed in three places, almost like the short joints in the leg of a crab. The joints of the limbs I could not see, because of the puttee-like straps in which they were swathed, and which formed the only clothing the being wore.

There the thing was, looking at us!

At the time my mind was taken up by the mad impossibility of the creature. I suppose he also was amazed, and with more reason, perhaps, for amazement than we. Only, confound him! he did not show it. We did at least know what had brought about this meeting of incompatible creatures. But conceive how it would seem to decent Londoners, for example, to come upon a couple of living things, as big as men and absolutely unlike any other earthly animals, careering about among the sheep in Hyde Park! It must have taken him like that.

Figure us! We were bound hand and foot, fagged and filthy; our beards two inches long, our faces scratched and bloody. Cavor you must imagine in his knickerbockers (torn in several places by the bayonet scrub) his Jaegar shirt and old cricket cap, his wiry hair wildly disordered, a tail to every quarter of the heavens. In that blue light his face did not look red but very dark, his lips and the drying blood upon my hands seemed black. If possible I was in a worse plight than he, on account of the yellow fungus into which I had jumped. Our jackets were unbuttoned, and our shoes had been taken off and lay at our feet. And we were sitting with our backs to this queer bluish light, peering at such a monster as Dürer might have invented.

Cavor broke the silence; started to speak, went hoarse, and cleared his throat. Outside began a terrific bellowing, as if a mooncalf were in trouble. It ended in a shriek, and everything was still again.

Presently the Selenite turned about, flickered into the shadow, stood for a moment retrospective at the door, and then closed it on us; and once more we were in that murmurous mystery of darkness into which we had awakened.

# CHAPTER THIRTEEN

## Mr Cavor Makes Some Suggestions

For a time neither of us spoke. To focus together all the things we had brought upon ourselves, seemed beyond my mental powers.

"They've got us," I said at last.

"It was that fungus."

"Well – if I hadn't taken it we should have fainted and starved."

"We might have found the sphere."

I lost my temper at his persistence, and swore to myself. For a time we hated one another in silence. I drummed with my fingers on the floor between my knees, and gritted the links of my fetters together. Presently I was forced to talk again.

"What do you make of it, anyhow?" I asked humbly.

"They are reasonable creatures – they can make things and do things – Those lights we saw…"

He stopped. It was clear he could make nothing of it.

When he spoke again it was to confess, "After all, they are more human than we had a right to expect. I suppose – "

He stopped irritatingly.

"Yes?"

"I suppose, anyhow – on any planet where there is an intelligent animal – it will carry its brain case upward, and have hands, and walk erect..."

Presently he broke away in another direction.

"We are some way in," he said. "I mean – perhaps a couple of thousand feet or more."

"Why?"

"It's cooler. And our voices are so much louder. That faded quality – it has altogether gone. And the feeling in one's ears and throat."

I had not noted that, but I did now.

"The air is denser. We must be some depths – a mile even, we may be – inside the moon."

"We never thought of a world inside the moon."

"No."

"How could we?"

"We might have done. Only – One gets into habits of mind."

He thought for a time.

"*Now*," he said, "it seems such an obvious thing.

"Of course! The moon must be enormously cavernous, with an atmosphere within, and at the centre of its caverns a sea.

"One knew that the moon had a lower specific gravity than the earth, one knew that it had little air or water outside, one knew, too, that it was sister planet to the earth, and that it was unaccountable that it should be different in composition. The inference that it was hollowed out was as clear as day. And yet one never saw it as a fact. Kepler, of course – "

His voice had the interest now of a man who has discovered a pretty sequence of reasoning.

"Yes," he said, "Kepler with his *sub-volvani* was right after all."

"I wish you had taken the trouble to find that out before we came," I said.

He answered nothing, buzzing to himself softly, as he pursued his thoughts. My temper was going.

"What do you think has become of the sphere, anyhow?" I asked.

"Lost," he said, like a man who answers an uninteresting question.

"Among those plants?"

"Unless they find it."

"And then?"

"How can I tell?"

"Cavor," I said, with a sort of hysterical bitterness, "things look bright for my Company..."

He made no answer.

"Good Lord!" I exclaimed. "Just think of all the trouble we took to get into this pickle! What did we come for? What are we after? What was the moon to us or we to the moon? We wanted too much, we tried too much. We ought to have started the little things first. It was you proposed the moon! Those Cavorite spring blinds! I am certain we could have worked them for terrestrial purposes. Certain! Did you really understand what I proposed? A steel cylinder – "

"Rubbish!" said Cavor.

We ceased to converse.

For a time Cavor kept up a broken monologue without much help from me.

"If they find it," he began, "if they find it…what will they do with it? Well, that's a question. It may be that's *the* question. They won't understand it, anyhow. If they understood that sort of thing they would have come long since to the earth. Would they? Why shouldn't they? But they would have sent something – They couldn't keep their hands off such a possibility. No! But they will examine it. Clearly they are intelligent and inquisitive. They will examine it – get inside it – trifle with the studs. Off!… That would mean the moon for us for all the rest of our lives. Strange creatures, strange knowledge…"

"As for strange knowledge – " said I, and language failed me.

"Look here, Bedford," said Cavor, "you came on this expedition of your own free will."

"You said to me, 'Call it prospecting'."

"There's always risks in prospecting."

"Especially when you do it unarmed and without thinking out every possibility."

"I was so taken up with the sphere. The thing rushed on us, and carried us away."

"Rushed on *me*, you mean."

"Rushed on me just as much. How was *I* to know when I set to work on molecular physics that the business would bring me here – of all places?"

"It's this accursed science," I cried. "It's the very Devil. The mediaeval priests and persecutors were right and the Moderns are all wrong. You tamper with it – and it offers you gifts. And directly you take them it knocks you to pieces in some unexpected way. Old passions and new weapons – now it upsets your religion, now it upsets your social ideas, now it whirls you off to desolation and misery!"

"Anyhow, it's no use your quarrelling with me *now*. These creatures – these Selenites, or whatever we choose to call them – have got us tied hand and foot. Whatever temper you choose to go through with it in, you will have to go through with it... We have experiences before us that will need all our coolness."

He paused as if he required my assent. But I sat sulking. "Confound your science!" I said.

"The problem is communication. Gestures, I fear, will be different. Pointing, for example. No creatures but men and monkeys point."

That was too obviously wrong for me. "Pretty nearly every animal," I cried, "points with its eyes or nose."

Cavor meditated over that. "Yes," he said at last, "and we don't. There's such differences – such differences!

"One might... But how can I tell? There is speech. The sounds they make, a sort of fluting and piping. I don't see how we are to imitate that. Is it their speech, that sort of thing? They may have different senses, different means of communication. Of course they are minds and we are minds; there must be something in common. Who knows how far we may not get to an understanding?"

"The things are outside us," I said. "They're more different from us than the strangest animals on earth. They are a different clay. What is the good of talking like this?"

Cavor thought. "I don't see that. Where there are minds they will have something *similar* – even though they have been evolved on different planets. Of course if it was a question of instincts, if we or they are no more than animals – "

"Well, *are* they? They're much more like ants on their hind legs than human beings, and who ever got to any sort of understanding with ants?"

"But these machines and clothing! No, I don't hold with you, Bedford. The difference is wide – "

"It's insurmountable."

"The resemblance must bridge it. I remember reading once a paper by the late Professor Galton on the possibility of communication between the planets. Unhappily, at that time it did not seem probable that that would be of any material benefit to me, and I fear I did not give it the attention I should have done – in view of this state of affairs. Yet... Now, let me see!

"His idea was to begin with those broad truths that must underlie all conceivable mental existences and establish a basis on those. The great principles of geometry, to begin with. He proposed to take some leading proposition of Euclid's, and show by construction that its truth was known to us, to demonstrate, for example, that the angles at the base of an isosceles triangle are equal, and that if the equal sides be produced the angles on the other side of the base are equal also, or that the square on the hypotenuse of a right-angled triangle is equal to the sum of the squares on the two other sides. By demonstrating our knowledge of these things we should demonstrate our possession of a reasonable intelligence... Now, suppose I... I might draw the geometrical figure with a wet finger, or even trace it in the air..."

He fell silent. I sat meditating his words. For a time his wild hope of communication, of interpretation, with these weird beings held me. Then that angry despair that was a part of my exhaustion and physical misery resumed its sway. I perceived with a sudden novel vividness the extraordinary folly of

112

everything I had ever done. "Ass!" I said; "oh, ass, unutterable ass... I seem to exist only to go about doing preposterous things. Why did we ever leave the thing?... Hopping about looking for patents and concessions in the craters of the moon!... If only we had had the sense to fasten a handkerchief to a stick to show where we had left the sphere!"

I subsided, fuming.

"It is clear," meditated Cavor, "they are intelligent. One can hypotheticate certain things. As they have not killed us at once, they must have ideas of mercy. Mercy! at any rate of restraint. Possibly of intercourse. They may meet us. And this apartment and the glimpses we had of its guardian. These fetters! A high degree of intelligence..."

"I wish to heaven," cried I, "I'd thought even twice! Plunge after plunge. First one fluky start and then another. It was my confidence in you! *Why* didn't I stick to my play? That was what I was equal to. That was my world and the life I was made for. I could have finished that play. I'm certain...it was a good play. I had the scenario as good as done. Then... Conceive it! leaping to the moon! Practically – I've thrown my life away! That old woman in the inn near Canterbury had better sense."

I looked up, and stopped in mid-sentence. The darkness had given place to that bluish light again. The door was opening, and several noiseless Selenites were coming into the chamber. I became quite still, staring at their grotesque faces.

Then suddenly my sense of disagreeable strangeness changed to interest. I perceived that the foremost and second carried bowls. One elemental need at least our minds could understand in common. They were bowls of some metal that, like our fetters, looked dark in that bluish light; and each contained a number of

113

whitish fragments. All the cloudy pain and misery that oppressed me rushed together and took the shape of hunger. I eyed these bowls wolfishly, and, though it returned to me in dreams, at that time it seemed a small matter that at the end of the arms that lowered one towards me were not hands, but a sort of flap and thumb, like the end of an elephant's trunk.

The stuff in the bowl was loose in texture, and whitish brown in colour – rather like lumps of some cold soufflé, and it smelt faintly like mushrooms. From a partially divided carcass of a mooncalf that we presently saw, I am inclined to believe it must have been mooncalf flesh.

My hands were so tightly chained that I could barely contrive to reach the bowl; but when they saw the effort I made, two of them dexterously released one of the turns about my wrist. Their tentacle hands were soft and cold to my skin. I immediately seized a mouthful of the food. It had the same laxness in texture that all organic structures seem to have upon the moon; it tasted rather like a gauffre or a damp meringue, but in no way was it disagreeable. I took two other mouthfuls. "I *wanted* – foo'!" said I, tearing off a still larger piece...

For a time we ate with an utter absence of self-consciousness. We ate and presently drank like tramps in a soup kitchen. Never before nor since have I been hungry to the ravenous pitch, and save that I have had this very experience I could never have believed that, a quarter of a million of miles out of our proper world, in utter perplexity of soul, surrounded, watched, touched by beings more grotesque and inhuman than the worst creations of a nightmare, it would be possible for me to eat in utter forgetfulness of all these things. They stood about us watching us, and ever and again making a slight elusive twittering that stood them, I suppose, in the stead of speech. I did not even shiver at their touch. And when the first zeal of my feeding was over, I could note that Cavor, too, had been eating with the same shameless abandon.

# CHAPTER FOURTEEN

## Experiments in Intercourse

When at last we had made an end of eating, the Selenites linked our hands closely together again, and then untwisted the chains about our feet and rebound them, so as to give us a limited freedom of movement. Then they unfastened the chains about our waists. To do all this they had to handle us freely, and ever and again one of their queer heads came down close to my face, or a soft tentacle-hand touched my head or neck. I don't remember that I was afraid then or repelled by their proximity. I think that our incurable anthropomorphism made us imagine there were human heads inside their masks. The skin, like everything else, looked bluish, but that was on account of the light; and it was hard and shiny, quite in the beetle-wing fashion, not soft, or moist, or hairy, as a vertebrated animal's would be. Along the crest of the head was a low ridge of whitish spines running from back to front, and a much larger ridge curved on either side over the eyes. The Selenite who untied me used his mouth to help his hands.

"They seem to be releasing us," said Cavor. "Remember we are on the moon! Make no sudden movements!"

"Are you going to try that geometry?"

"If I get a chance. But, of course, they may make an advance first."

We remained passive, and the Selenites, having finished their arrangements, stood back from us, and seemed to be looking at us. I say seemed to be, because as their eyes were at the side and not in front, one had the same difficulty in determining the direction in which they were looking as one has in the case of a hen or a fish. They conversed with one another in their reedy tones, that seemed to me impossible to imitate or define. The door behind us opened wider, and, glancing over my shoulder, I saw a vague large space beyond, in which quite a little crowd of Selenites were standing. They seemed a curiously miscellaneous rabble.

"Do they want us to imitate those sounds?" I asked Cavor.

"I don't think so," he said.

"It seems to me that they are trying to make us understand something."

"I can't make anything of their gestures. Do you notice this one, who is worrying with his head like a man with an uncomfortable collar?"

"Let us shake our heads at him."

We did that, and finding it ineffectual, attempted an imitation of the Selenites' movements. That seemed to interest them. At any rate they all set up the same movement. But as that seemed to lead to nothing, we desisted at last and so did they, and fell into a piping argument among themselves. Then one of them, shorter and very much thicker than the others, and with a particularly wide mouth, squatted down suddenly beside Cavor, and put his hands and feet in the same posture as Cavor's were bound, and then by a dexterous movement stood up.

"Cavor," I shouted, "they want us to get up!"

118

He stared open-mouthed. "That's it!" he said.

And with much heaving and grunting, because our hands were tied together, we contrived to struggle to our feet. The Selenites made way for our elephantine heavings, and seemed to twitter more volubly. As soon as we were on our feet the thick-set Selenite came and patted each of our faces with his tentacles, and walked towards the open doorway. That also was plain enough, and we followed him. We saw that four of the Selenites standing in the doorway were much taller than the others, and clothed in the same manner as those we had seen in the crater, namely, with spiked round helmets and cylindrical body-cases, and that each of the four carried a goad with spike and guard made of that same dull-looking metal as the bowls. These four closed about us, one on either side of each of us, as we emerged from our chamber into the cavern from which the light had come.

We did not get our impression of that cavern all at once. Our attention was taken up by the movements and attitudes of the Selenites immediately about us, and by the necessity of controlling our motion, lest we should startle and alarm them and ourselves by some excessive stride. In front of us was the short, thick-set being who had solved the problem of asking us to get up, moving with gestures that seemed, almost all of them, intelligible to us, inviting us to follow him. His spout-like face turned from one of us to the other with a quickness that was clearly interrogative. For a time, I say, we were taken up with these things.

But at last the great place that formed a background to our movements asserted itself. It became apparent that the source of much, at least, of the tumult of sounds which had filled our ears ever since we had recovered from the stupefaction of the fungus

119

was a vast mass of machinery in active movement, whose flying and whirling parts were visible indistinctly over the heads and between the bodies of the Selenites who walked about us. And not only did the web of sounds that filled the air proceed from this mechanism, but also the peculiar blue light that irradiated the whole place. We had taken it as a natural thing that a subterranean cavern should be artificially lit, and even now, though the fact was patent to my eyes, I did not really grasp its import until presently the darkness came. The meaning and structure of this huge apparatus we saw I cannot explain, because we neither of us learnt what it was for or how it worked. One after another, big shafts of metal flung out and up from its centre, their heads travelling in what seemed to me to be a parabolic path; each dropped a sort of dangling arm as it rose towards the apex of its flight and plunged down into a vertical cylinder, forcing this down before it. About it moved the shapes of tenders, little figures that seemed vaguely different from the beings about us. As each of the three dangling arms of the machine plunged down, there was a clank and then a roaring, and out of the top of the vertical cylinder came pouring this incandescent substance that lit the place, and ran over as milk runs over a boiling pot, and dripped luminously into a tank of light below. It was a cold blue light, a sort of phosphorescent glow but infinitely brighter, and from the tanks into which it fell it ran in conduits athwart the cavern.

Thud, thud, thud, thud, came the sweeping arms of this unintelligible apparatus, and the light substance hissed and poured. At first the thing seemed only reasonably large and near to us, and then I saw how exceedingly little the Selenites upon it seemed, and I realised the full immensity of cavern and machine.

I looked from this tremendous affair to the faces of the Selenites with a new respect. I stopped, and Cavor stopped, and stared at this thunderous engine.

"But this is stupendous!" I said. "What can it be for?"

Cavor's blue-lit face was full of an intelligent respect. "I can't dream! Surely these beings – Men could not make a thing like that! Look at those arms, are they on connecting rods?"

The thick-set Selenite had gone some paces unheeded. He came back and stood between us and the great machine. I avoided seeing him, because I guessed somehow that his idea was to beckon us onward. He walked away in the direction he wished us to go, and turned and came back, and flicked our faces to attract our attention.

Cavor and I looked at one another.

"Cannot we show him we are interested in the machine?" I said.

"Yes," said Cavor. "We'll try that." He turned to our guide and smiled, and pointed to the machine, and pointed again, and then to his head, and then to the machine. By some defect of reasoning he seemed to imagine that broken English might help these gestures. "Me look 'im," he said, "me think 'im very much. Yes."

His behaviour seemed to check the Selenites in their desire for our progress for a moment. They faced one another, their queer heads moved, the twittering voices came quick and liquid. Then one of them, a lean, tall creature, with a sort of mantle added to the puttee in which the others were dressed, twisted his elephant trunk of a hand about Cavor's waist, and pulled him gently to follow our guide, who again went on ahead.

Cavor resisted. "We may just as well begin explaining ourselves now. They may think we are new animals, a new sort of mooncalf perhaps! It is most important that we should show an intelligent interest from the outset."

He began to shake his head violently. "No, no," he said, "me not come on one minute. Me look at 'im."

"Isn't there some geometrical point you might bring in apropos of that affair?" I suggested, as the Selenites conferred again.

"Possibly a parabolic – " he began.

He yelled loudly, and leaped six feet or more!

One of the four armed moon-men had pricked him with a goad!

I turned on the goad-bearer behind me with a swift threatening gesture, and he started back. This and Cavor's sudden shout and leap clearly astonished all the Selenites. They receded hastily, facing us. For one of those moments that seem to last for ever, we stood in angry protest, with a scattered semicircle of these inhuman beings about us.

"He pricked me!" said Cavor, with a catching of the voice.

"I saw him," I answered.

"Confound it!" I said to the Selenites; "we're not going to stand that! What on earth do you take us for?"

I glanced quickly right and left. Far away across the blue wilderness of cavern I saw a number of other Selenites running towards us; broad and slender they were, and one with a larger head than the others. The cavern spread wide and low, and receded in every direction into darkness. Its roof, I remember, seemed to bulge down as if with the weight of the vast thickness of rocks that prisoned us. There was no way out of it – no way out of it. Above, below, in every direction, was the unknown, and these inhuman creatures, with goads and gestures, confronting us, and we two unsupported men!

# CHAPTER FIFTEEN

## The Giddy Bridge

J ust for a moment that hostile pause endured. I suppose that both we and the Selenites did some very rapid thinking. My clearest impression was that there was nothing to put my back against, and that we were bound to be surrounded and killed. The overwhelming folly of our presence there loomed over me in black, enormous reproach. Why had I ever launched myself on this mad, inhuman expedition?

Cavor came to my side and laid his hand on my arm. His pale and terrified face was ghastly in the blue light.

"We can't do anything," he said. "It's a mistake. They don't understand. We must go. As they want us to go."

I looked down at him, and then at the fresh Selenites who were coming to help their fellows. "If I had my hands free – "

"It's no use," he panted.

"No."

"We'll go."

And he turned about and led the way in the direction that had been indicated for us.

I followed, trying to look as subdued as possible, and feeling at the chains about my wrists. My blood was boiling. I noted nothing more of that cavern, though it seemed to take a long time before we had marched across it, or if I noted anything I forgot it as I saw it. My thoughts were concentrated, I think, upon my chains and the Selenites, and particularly upon the helmeted ones with the goads. At first they marched parallel with us, and at a respectful distance, but presently they were overtaken by three others, and then they drew nearer, until they were within arm's length again. I winced like a beaten horse as they came near to us. The shorter, thicker Selenite marched at first on our right flank, but presently came in front of us again.

How well the picture of that grouping has bitten into my brain; the back of Cavor's downcast head just in front of me, and the dejected droop of his shoulders, and our guide's gaping visage, perpetually jerking about him, and the goad-bearers on either side, watchful, yet open-mouthed – a blue monochrome. And after all, I *do* remember one other thing besides the purely personal affair, which is, that a sort of gutter came presently across the floor of the cavern, and then ran along by the side of the path of rock we followed. And it was full of that same bright blue luminous stuff that flowed out of the great machine. I walked close beside it, and I can testify it radiated not a particle of heat. It was brightly shining, and yet it was neither warmer nor colder than anything else in the cavern.

Clang, clang, clang, we passed right under the thumping levers of another vast machine, and so came at last to a wide tunnel, in which we could even hear the pad, pad, of our shoeless feet, and which, save for the trickling thread of blue to the right of us, was quite unlit. The shadows made gigantic travesties of our shapes and those of the Selenites on the irregular wall and roof of the tunnel. Ever and again crystals in the walls of the tunnel

124

scintillated like gems, ever and again the tunnel expanded into a stalactitic cavern, or gave off branches that vanished into darkness.

We seemed to be marching down that tunnel for a long time. "Trickle, trickle," went the flowing light very softly, and our footfalls and their echoes made an irregular paddle, paddle. My mind settled down to the question of my chains. If I were to slip off one turn *so*, and then to twist it *so*...

If I tried to do it very gradually, would they see I was slipping my wrist out of the looser turn? If they did, what would they do?

"Bedford," said Cavor, "it goes down. It keeps on going down."

His remark roused me from my sullen preoccupation.

"If they wanted to kill us," he said, dropping back to come level with me, "there is no reason why they should not have done it."

"No," I admitted, "that's true."

"They don't understand us," he said, "they think we are merely strange animals, some wild sort of mooncalf birth, perhaps. It will be only when they have observed us better that they will begin to think we have minds – "

"When you trace those geometrical problems," said I.

"It may be that."

We tramped on for a space.

"You see," said Cavor, "these may be Selenites of a lower class."

"The infernal fools!" said I viciously, glancing at their exasperating faces.

"If we endure what they do to us – "

"We've got to endure it," said I.

"There may be others less stupid. This is the mere outer fringe of their world. It must go down and down, cavern, passage, tunnel, down at last to the sea – hundreds of miles below."

His words made me think of the mile or so of rock and tunnel that might be over our heads already. It was like a weight dropping, on my shoulders. "Away from the sun and air," I said. "Even a mine half a mile deep is stuffy."

"This is not, anyhow. It's probable – Ventilation! The air would blow from the dark side of the moon to the sunlit, and all the carbonic acid would well out there and feed those plants. Up this tunnel, for example, there is quite a breeze. And what a world it must be. The earnest we have in that shaft, and those machines – "

"And the goad," I said. "Don't forget the goad!"

He walked a little in front of me for a time.

"Even that goad – " he said.

"Well?"

"I was angry at the time. But – It was perhaps necessary we should get on. They have different skins, and probably different nerves. They may not understand our objection – Just as a being from Mars might not like our earthly habit of nudging – "

"They'd better be careful how they nudge *me*."

"And about that geometry. After all, their way is a way of understanding, too. They begin with the elements of life and not of thought. Food. Compulsion. Pain. They strike at fundamentals."

"There's no doubt about *that*," I said.

He went on to talk of the enormous and wonderful world into which we were being taken. I realised slowly from his tone, that even now he was not absolutely in despair at the prospect of going ever deeper into this inhuman planet-burrow. His mind ran on machines and invention, to the exclusion of a thousand dark things that beset me. It wasn't that he intended to make any use of these things, he simply wanted to know them.

"After all," he said, "this is a tremendous occasion. It is the meeting of two worlds! What are we going to see? Think of what is below us here."

"We shan't see much if the light isn't better," I remarked.

"This is only the outer crust. Down below – On this scale – There will be everything. Do you notice how different they seem one from another? The story we shall take back!"

"Some rare sort of animal," I said, "might comfort himself in that way while they were bringing him to the Zoo... It doesn't follow that we are going to be shown all these things."

"When they find we have reasonable minds," said Cavor, "they will want to learn about the earth. Even if they have no generous emotions, they will teach in order to learn... And the things they must know! The unanticipated things!"

He went on to speculate on the possibility of their knowing things he had never hoped to learn on earth, speculating in that way, with a raw wound from that goad already in his skin! Much that he said I forget, for my attention was drawn to the fact that the tunnel along which we had been marching was opening out wider and wider. We seemed, from the feeling of the air, to be going out into a huge space. But how big the space might really be we could not tell, because it was unlit. Our little stream of light ran in a dwindling thread and vanished far ahead. Presently the rocky walls had vanished altogether on either hand. There was nothing to be seen but the path in front of us and the trickling hurrying rivulet

127

of blue phosphorescence. The figures of Cavor and the guiding Selenite marched before me, the sides of their legs and heads that were towards the rivulet were clear and bright blue, their darkened sides, now that the reflection of the tunnel wall no longer lit them, merged indistinguishably in the darkness beyond.

And soon I perceived that we were approaching a declivity of some sort, because the little blue stream dipped suddenly out of sight.

In another moment, as it seemed, we had reached the edge. The shining stream gave one meander of hesitation and then rushed over. It fell to a depth at which the sound of its descent was absolutely lost to us. Far below was a bluish glow, a sort of blue mist – at an infinite distance below. And the darkness the stream dropped out of became utterly void and black, save that a thing like a plank projected from the edge of the cliff and stretched out and faded and vanished altogether. There was a warm air blowing up out of the gulf.

For a moment I and Cavor stood as near the edge as we dared, peering into a blue-tinged profundity. And then our guide was pulling at my arm.

Then he left me, and walked to the end of that plank and stepped upon it, looking back. Then when he perceived we watched him, he turned about and went on along it, walking as surely as though he was on firm earth. For a moment his form was distinct, then he became a blue blur, and then vanished into the obscurity. I became aware of some vague shape looming darkly out of the black.

There was a pause. "Surely – !" said Cavor.

One of the other Selenites walked a few paces out upon the plank, and turned and looked back at us unconcernedly. The others stood ready to follow after us. Our guide's expectant figure reappeared. He was returning to see why we had not advanced.

"What is that beyond there?" I asked.

"I can't see."

"We can't cross this at any price," said I.

"I could not go three steps on it," said Cavor, "even with my hands free."

We looked at each other's drawn faces in blank consternation.

"They can't know what it is to be giddy!" said Cavor.

"It's quite impossible for us to walk that plank."

"I don't believe they see as we do. I've been watching them. I wonder if they know this is simply blackness for us. How can we make them understand?"

"Anyhow, we must make them understand."

I think we said these things with a vague half hope the Selenites might somehow understand. I knew quite clearly that all that was needed was an explanation. Then as I saw their faces, I realised that an explanation was impossible. Just here it was that our resemblances were not going to bridge our differences. Well, I wasn't going to walk the plank, anyhow. I slipped my wrist very quickly out of the coil of chain that was loose, and then began to twist my wrists in opposite directions. I was standing nearest to the bridge, and as I did this two of the Selenites laid hold of me, and pulled me gently towards it.

I shook my head violently. "No go," I said, "no use. You don't understand."

Another Selenite added his compulsion. I was forced to step forward.

"I've got an idea," said Cavor; but I knew his ideas.

"Look here!" I exclaimed to the Selenites. "Steady on! It's all very well for you – "

I sprang round upon my heel. I burst out into curses. For one of the armed Selenites had stabbed me behind with his goad.

I wrenched my wrists free from the little tentacles that held them. I turned on the goad-bearer. "Confound you!" I cried. "I've warned you of that. What on earth do you think I'm made of, to stick that into me? If you touch me again – "

By way of answer he pricked me forthwith.

I heard Cavor's voice in alarm and entreaty. Even then I think he wanted to compromise with these creatures. "I say, Bedford," he cried, "I know a way!" But the sting of that second stab seemed to set free some pent-up reserve of energy in my being. Instantly the link of the wrist-chain snapped, and with it snapped all considerations that had held us unresisting in the hands of these moon creatures. For that second, at least, I was mad with fear and anger. I took no thought of consequences. I hit straight out at the face of the thing with the goad. The chain was twisted round my fist...

There came another of these beastly surprises of which the moon world is full.

My mailed hand seemed to go clean through him. He smashed like – like some softish sort of sweet with liquid in it! He broke right in! He squelched and splashed. It was like hitting a damp toadstool. The flimsy body went spinning a dozen yards, and fell with a flabby impact. I was astonished. I was incredulous that any living thing could be so flimsy. For an instant I could have believed the whole thing a dream.

Then it had become real and imminent again. Neither Cavor nor the other Selenites seemed to have done anything from the time when I had turned about to the time when the dead Selenite hit the ground. Everyone stood back from us two, everyone alert. That arrest seemed to last at least a second after the Selenite was down. Everyone must have been taking the thing in. I seem to remember myself standing with my arm half retracted, trying also to take it in. "What next?" clamoured my brain; "what next?" Then in a moment everyone was moving!

I perceived we must get our chains loose, and that before we could do this these Selenites had to be beaten off. I faced towards the group of the three goad-bearers. Instantly one threw his goad at me. It swished over my head, and I suppose went flying into the abyss behind.

I leaped right at him with all my might as the goad flew over me. He turned to run as I jumped, and I bore him to the ground, came down right upon him, and slipped upon his smashed body and fell. He seemed to wriggle under my foot.

I came into a sitting position, and on every hand the blue backs of the Selenites were receding into the darkness. I bent a link by main force and untwisted the chain that had hampered me about the ankles, and sprang to my feet, with the chain in my hand. Another goad, flung javelin-wise, whistled by me, and I made a rush towards the darkness out of which it had come. Then I turned back towards Cavor, who was still standing in the light of the rivulet near the gulf convulsively busy with his wrists, and at the same time jabbering nonsense about his idea.

"Come on!" I cried.

"My hands!" he answered.

Then, realising that I dared not run back to him, because my ill-calculated steps might carry me over the edge, he came shuffling towards me, with his hands held out before him.

131

I gripped his chains at once to unfasten them.

"Where are they?" he panted.

"Run away. They'll come back. They're throwing things! Which way shall we go?"

"By the light. To that tunnel. Eh?"

"Yes," said I, and his hands were free.

I dropped on my knees and fell to work on his ankle bonds. Whack came something – I know not what – and splashed the livid streamlet into drops about us. Far away on our right a piping and whistling began.

I whipped the chain off his feet, and put it in his hand. "Hit with that!" I said, and without waiting for an answer, set off in big bounds along the path by which we had come. I had a nasty sort of feeling that these things could jump out of the darkness onto my back. I heard the impact of his leaps come following after me.

We ran in vast strides. But that running, you must understand, was an altogether different thing from any running on earth. On earth one leaps and almost instantly hits the ground again, but on the moon, because of its weaker pull, one shot through the air for several seconds before one came to earth. In spite of our violent hurry this gave an effect of long pauses, pauses in which one might have counted seven or eight. "Step," and one soared off! All sorts of questions ran through my mind: "Where are the Selenites? What will they do? Shall we ever get to that tunnel? Is Cavor far behind? Are they likely to cut him off?" Then whack, stride, and off again for another step.

I saw a Selenite running in front of me, his legs going exactly as a man's would go on earth, saw him glance over his shoulder, and heard him shriek as he ran aside out of my way into the darkness. He was, I think, our guide, but I am not sure. Then in another vast stride the walls of rock had come into view on either hand, and in two more strides I was in the tunnel, and tempering my pace to its low roof. I went onto a bend, then stopped and turned back, and plug, plug, plug, Cavor came into view, splashing into the stream of blue light at every stride, and grew larger and blundered into me. We stood clutching each other. For a moment, at least, we had shaken off our captors and were alone.

We were both very much out of breath. We spoke in panting, broken sentences.

"You've spoilt it all!" panted Cavor.

"Nonsense," I cried. "It was that or death!"

"What are we to do?"

"Hide."

"How can we?"

"It's dark enough."

"But where?"

"Up one of these side caverns."

"And then?"

"Think."

"Right – come on."

We strode on, and presently came to a radiating dark cavern. Cavor was in front. He hesitated, and chose a black mouth that seemed to promise good hiding. He went towards it and turned.

"It's dark," he said.

"Your legs and feet will light us. You're wet with that luminous stuff."

"But – "

A tumult of sounds, and in particular a sound like a clanging gong, advancing up the main tunnel, became audible. It was horribly suggestive of a tumultuous pursuit. We made a bolt for the unlit side cavern forthwith. As we ran along it our way was lit by the irradiation of Cavor's legs. "It's lucky," I panted, "they took off our boots, or we should fill this place with clatter." On we rushed, taking as small steps as we could to avoid striking the roof of the cavern. After a time we seemed to be gaining on the uproar. It became muffled, it dwindled, it died away.

I stopped and looked back, and I heard the pad, pad of Cavor's feet receding. Then he stopped also. "Bedford," he whispered; "there's a sort of light in front of us."

I looked, and at first could see nothing. Then I perceived his head and shoulders dimly outlined against a fainter darkness. I saw, also, that this mitigation of the darkness was not blue, as all the other light within the moon had been, but a pallid gray, a very vague, faint white, the daylight colour. Cavor noted this difference as soon, or sooner, than I did, and I think, too, that it filled him with much the same wild hope.

"Bedford," he whispered, and his voice trembled. "That light – it is possible – "

He did not dare to say the thing he hoped. Then came a pause. Suddenly I knew by the sound of his feet that he was striding towards that pallor. I followed him with a beating heart.

# Chapter Sixteen

## Points of View

The light grew stronger as we advanced. In a little time it was nearly as strong as the phosphorescence on Cavor's legs. Our tunnel was expanding into a cavern, and this new light was at the farther end of it. I perceived something that set my hopes leaping and bounding.

"Cavor," I said, "it comes from above! I am certain it comes from above!"

He made no answer, but hurried on.

Indisputably it was a gray light, a silvery light.

In another moment we were beneath it. It filtered down through a chink in the walls of the cavern, and as I stared up, drip, came a drop of water upon my face. I started and stood aside – drip, fell another drop quite audibly on the rocky floor.

"Cavor," I said, "if one of us lifts the other, he can reach that crack!"

"I'll lift you," he said, and incontinently hoisted me as though I was a baby.

I thrust an arm into the crack, and just at my fingertips found a little ledge by which I could hold. I could see the white light was very much brighter now. I pulled myself up by two fingers with scarcely an effort, though on earth I weigh twelve stone, reached to a still higher corner of rock, and so got my feet on the narrow ledge. I stood up and searched up the rocks with my fingers; the cleft broadened out upwardly. "It's climbable," I said to Cavor. "Can you jump up to my hand if I hold it down to you?"

I wedged myself between the sides of the cleft, rested knee and foot on the ledge, and extended a hand. I could not see Cavor, but I could hear the rustle of his movements as he crouched to spring. Then whack and he was hanging to my arm – and no heavier than a kitten! I lugged him up until he had a hand on my ledge, and could release me.

"Confound it!" I said, "anyone could be a mountaineer on the moon;" and so set myself in earnest to the climbing. For a few minutes I clambered steadily, and then I looked up again. The cleft opened out steadily, and the light was brighter. Only –

It was not daylight after all.

In another moment I could see what it was, and at the sight I could have beaten my head against the rocks with disappointment. For I beheld simply an irregularly sloping open space, and all over its slanting floor stood a forest of little club-shaped fungi, each shining gloriously with that pinkish silvery light. For a moment I stared at their soft radiance, then sprang forward and upward among them. I plucked up half a dozen and flung them against the rocks, and then sat down, laughing bitterly, as Cavor's ruddy face came into view.

"It's phosphorescence again!" I said. "No need to hurry. Sit down and make yourself at home." And as he spluttered over our disappointment, I began to lob more of these growths into the cleft.

"I thought it was daylight," he said.

"Daylight!" cried I. "Daybreak, sunset, clouds, and windy skies! Shall we ever see such things again?"

As I spoke, a little picture of our world seemed to rise before me, bright and little and clear, like the background of some old Italian picture. "The sky that changes, and the sea that changes, and the hills and the green trees and the towns and cities shining in the sun. Think of a wet roof at sunset, Cavor! Think of the windows of a westward house!" He made no answer.

"Here we are burrowing in this beastly world that isn't a world, with its inky ocean hidden in some abominable blackness below, and outside that torrid day and that death stillness of night. And all these things that are chasing us now, beastly men of leather – insect men, that come out of a nightmare! After all, they're right! What business have we here smashing them and disturbing their world! For all we know the whole planet is up and after us already. In a minute we may hear them whimpering, and their gongs going. What are we to do? Where are we to go? Here we are as comfortable as snakes from Jamrach's loose in a Surbiton villa!"

"It was your fault," said Cavor.

"My fault!" I shouted. "Good Lord!"

"I had an idea!"

"Curse your ideas!"

"If we had refused to budge – "

"Under those goads?"

"Yes. They would have carried us!"

"Over that bridge?"

"Yes. They must have carried us from outside."

"I'd rather be carried by a fly across a ceiling."

"Good Heavens!"

I resumed my destruction of the fungi. Then suddenly I saw something that struck me even then.

"Cavor," I said, "these chains are of gold!"

He was thinking intently, with his hands gripping his cheeks. He turned his head slowly and stared at me, and when I had repeated my words, at the twisted chain about his right hand. "So they are," he said, "so they are." His face lost its transitory interest even as he looked. He hesitated for a moment, then went on with his interrupted meditation. I sat for a space puzzling over the fact that I had only just observed this, until I considered the blue light in which we had been, and which had taken all the colour out of the metal. And from that discovery I also started upon a train of thought that carried me wide and far. I forgot that I had just been asking what business we had in the moon. Gold –

It was Cavor who spoke first. "It seems to me that there are two courses open to us."

"Well."

"Either we can attempt to make our way – fight our way if necessary – out to the exterior again, and then hunt for our sphere until we find it, or the cold of the night comes to kill us, or else – "

He paused. "Yes?" I said, though I knew what was coming.

"We might attempt once more to establish some sort of understanding with the minds of the people in the moon."

"So far as I'm concerned – it's the first."

"I doubt."

"I don't."

"You see," said Cavor, "I do not think we can judge the Selenites by what we have seen of them. Their central world, their civilised world will be far below in the profounder caverns about their sea. This region of the crust in which we are is an outlying district, a pastoral region. At any rate, that is my interpretation. These Selenites we have seen may be only the equivalent of cowboys and engine-tenders. Their use of goads – in all probability mooncalf goads – the lack of imagination they show in expecting us to be able to do just what they can do, their indisputable brutality, all seem to point to something of that sort. But if we endured – "

"Neither of us could endure a six-inch plank across the bottomless pit for very long."

"No," said Cavor; "but then – "

"I *won't*," I said.

He discovered a new line of possibilities. "Well, suppose we got ourselves into some corner, where we could defend ourselves against these hinds and labourers. If, for example, we could hold out for a week or so, it is probable that the news of our appearance would filter down to the more intelligent and populous parts – "

"If they exist."

"They must exist, or whence came those tremendous machines?"

"That's possible, but it's the worst of the two chances."

"We might write up inscriptions on walls – "

"How do we know their eyes would see the sort of marks we made?"

"If we cut them – "

"That's possible, of course."

139

I took up a new thread of thought. "After all," I said, "I suppose you don't think these Selenites so infinitely wiser than men."

"They must know a lot more – or at least a lot of different things."

"Yes, but – " I hesitated.

"I think you'll quite admit, Cavor, that you're rather an exceptional man."

"How?"

"Well, you – you're a rather lonely man – have been, that is. You haven't married."

"Never wanted to. But why – "

"And you never grew richer than you happened to be?"

"Never wanted that either."

"You've just rooted after knowledge?"

"Well, a certain curiosity is natural – "

"You think so. That's just it. You think every other mind wants to *know*. I remember once, when I asked you why you conducted all these researches, you said you wanted your FRS, and to have the stuff called Cavorite, and things like that. You know perfectly well you didn't do it for that; but at the time my question took you by surprise, and you felt you ought to have something to look like a motive. Really you conducted researches because you *had* to. It's your twist."

"Perhaps it is – "

"It isn't one man in a million has that twist. Most men want – well, various things, but very few want knowledge for its own sake. *I* don't, I know perfectly well. Now, these Selenites seem to be a driving, busy sort of being, but how do you know that even the most intelligent will take an interest in us or our world? I don't believe they'll even know we have a world. They never come out at night – they'd freeze if they did. They've probably never seen any heavenly body at all except the blazing sun. How are they to know there is another world? What does it matter to them if they do? Well, even if they *have* had a glimpse of a few stars, or even of the earth crescent, what of that? Why should people living *inside* a planet trouble to observe that sort of thing? Men wouldn't have done it except for the seasons and sailing; why should the moon people?...

"Well, suppose there are a few philosophers like yourself. They are just the very Selenites who'll never have heard of our existence. Suppose a Selenite had dropped on the earth when you were at Lympne, you'd have been the last man in the world to hear he had come. You never read a newspaper! You see the chances against you. Well, it's for these chances we're sitting here doing nothing while precious time is flying. I tell you we've got into a fix. We've come unarmed, we've lost our sphere, we've got no food, we've shown ourselves to the Selenites, and made them think we're strange, strong, dangerous animals; and unless these Selenites are perfect fools, they'll set about now and hunt us till they find us, and when they find us they'll try to take us if they can, and kill us if they can't, and that's the end of the matter. If they take us, they'll probably kill us, through some misunderstanding. After we're done for, they may discuss us perhaps, but we shan't get much fun out of that."

"Go on."

"On the other hand, here's gold knocking about like cast iron at home. If only we can get some of it back, if only we can find our sphere again before they do, and get back, then – "

"Yes?"

141

"We might put the thing on a sounder footing. Come back in a bigger sphere with guns."

"Good Lord!" cried Cavor, as though that was horrible.

I shied another luminous fungus down the cleft.

"Look here, Cavor," I said, "I've half the voting power anyhow in this affair, and this is a case for a practical man. I'm a practical man, and you are not. I'm not going to trust to Selenites and geometrical diagrams if I can help it... That's all. Get back. Drop all this secrecy – or most of it. And come again."

He reflected. "When I came to the moon," he said, "I ought to have come alone."

"The question before the meeting," I said, "is how to get back to the sphere."

For a time we nursed our knees in silence. Then he seemed to decide for my reasons.

"I think," he said, "one can get data. It is clear that while the sun is on this side of the moon the air will be blowing through this planet sponge from the dark side hither. On this side, at any rate, the air will be expanding and flowing out of the moon caverns into the craters... Very well, there's a draught here."

"So there is."

"And that means that this is not a dead end; somewhere behind us this cleft goes on and up. The draught is blowing up, and that is the way we have to go. If we try to get up any sort of chimney or gully there is, we shall not only get out of these passages where they are hunting for us – "

"But suppose the gully is too narrow?"

"We'll come down again."

"Ssh!" I said suddenly; "what's that?"

142

We listened. At first it was an indistinct murmur, and then one picked out the clang of a gong. "They must think we are mooncalves," said I, "to be frightened at that."

"They're coming along that passage," said Cavor.

"They must be."

"They'll not think of the cleft. They'll go past."

I listened again for a space. "This time," I whispered, "they're likely to have some sort of weapon."

Then suddenly I sprang to my feet. "Good heavens, Cavor!" I cried. "But they *will!* They'll see the fungi I have been pitching down. They'll – !"

I didn't finish my sentence. I turned about and made a leap over the fungus tops towards the upper end of the cavity. I saw that the space turned upward and became a draughty cleft again, ascending to impenetrable darkness. I was about to clamber up into this, and then with a happy inspiration turned back.

"What are you doing?" asked Cavor.

"Go on!" said I, and went back and got two of the shining fungi, and putting one into the breast pocket of my flannel jacket, so that it stuck out to light our climbing, went back with the other for Cavor. The noise of the Selenites was now so loud that it seemed they must be already beneath the cleft. But it might be they would have difficulty in clambering into it, or might hesitate to ascend it against our possible resistance. At any rate, we had now the comforting knowledge of the enormous muscular superiority our birth in another planet gave us. In another minute I was clambering with gigantic vigour after Cavor's blue-lit heels.

# CHAPTER SEVENTEEN

## The Fight in the Cave of the Moon Butchers

I do not know how far we clambered before we came to the grating. It may be we ascended only a few hundred feet, but at the time it seemed to me we might have hauled and jammed and hopped and wedged ourselves through a mile or more of vertical ascent. Whenever I recall that time, there comes into my head the heavy clank of our golden chains that followed every movement. Very soon my knuckles and knees were raw, and I had a bruise on one cheek. After a time the first violence of our efforts diminished, and our movements became more deliberate and less painful. The noise of the pursuing Selenites had died away altogether. It seemed almost as though they had not traced us up the crack after all, in spite of the tell-tale heap of broken fungi that must have lain beneath it. At times the cleft narrowed so much that we could scarce squeeze up it; at others it expanded into great drusy cavities, studded with prickly crystals or thickly beset with dull, shining fungoid pimples. Sometimes it twisted spirally, and at other times slanted down nearly to the horizontal direction. Ever and again there was the intermittent drip and trickle of water by us. Once or twice it seemed to us that small living things had rustled out of our reach, but what they were we never saw. They may have been venomous beasts for all I know, but they did us no harm, and we were now tuned to a pitch when a weird creeping thing more or less mattered little. And at last, far above, came the familiar bluish light again, and then we saw that it filtered through a grating that barred our way.

We whispered as we pointed this out to one another, and became more and more cautious in our ascent. Presently we were close under the grating, and by pressing my face against its bars I could see a limited portion of the cavern beyond. It was clearly a large space, and lit no doubt by some rivulet of the same blue light that we had seen flow from the beating machinery. An intermittent trickle of water dropped ever and again between the bars near my face.

My first endeavour was naturally to see what might be upon the floor of the cavern, but our grating lay in a depression whose rim hid all this from our eyes. Our foiled attention then fell back upon the suggestion of the various sounds we heard, and presently my eye caught a number of faint shadows that played across the dim roof far overhead.

Indisputably there were several Selenites, perhaps a considerable number, in this space, for we could hear the noises of their intercourse, and faint sounds that I identified as their footfalls. There was also a succession of regularly repeated sounds – chid, chid, chid – which began and ceased, suggestive of a knife or spade hacking at some soft substance. Then came a clank as if of chains, a whistle and a rumble as of a truck running over a hollowed place, and then again that chid, chid, chid resumed. The shadows told of shapes that moved quickly and rhythmically, in agreement with that regular sound, and rested when it ceased.

We put our heads close together, and began to discuss these things in noiseless whispers.

"They are occupied," I said, "they are occupied in some way."

"Yes."

"They're not seeking us, or thinking of us."

"Perhaps they have not heard of us."

"Those others are hunting about below. If suddenly we appeared here – "

We looked at one another.

"There might be a chance to parley," said Cavor.

"No," I said. "Not as we are."

For a space we remained, each occupied by his own thoughts.

Chid, chid, chid went the chopping, and the shadows moved to and fro.

I looked at the grating. "It's flimsy," I said. "We might bend two of the bars and crawl through."

We wasted a little time in vague discussion. Then I took one of the bars in both hands, and got my feet up against the rock until they were almost on a level with my head, and so thrust against the bar. It bent so suddenly that I almost slipped. I clambered about and bent the adjacent bar in the opposite direction, and then took the luminous fungus from my pocket and dropped it down the fissure.

"Don't do anything hastily," whispered Cavor, as I twisted myself up through the opening I had enlarged. I had a glimpse of busy figures as I came through the grating, and immediately bent down, so that the rim of the depression in which the grating lay hid me from their eyes, and so lay flat, signalling advice to Cavor as he also prepared to come through. Presently we were

147

side by side in the depression, peering over the edge at the cavern and its occupants.

It was a much larger cavern than we had supposed from our first glimpse of it, and we looked up from the lowest portion of its sloping floor. It widened out as it receded from us, and its roof came down and hid the remoter portion altogether. And lying in a line along its length, vanishing at last far away in that tremendous perspective, were a number of huge shapes, huge pallid hulls, upon which the Selenites were busy. At first they seemed big white cylinders of vague import. Then I noted the heads upon them lying towards us, eyeless and skinless like the heads of sheep at a butcher's, and perceived they were the carcasses of mooncalves being cut up, much as the crew of a whaler might cut up a moored whale. They were cutting off the flesh in strips, and on some of the farther trunks the white ribs were showing. It was the sound of their hatchets that made that chid, chid. Some way away a thing like a trolley cable, drawn and loaded with chunks of lax meat, was running up the slope of the cavern floor. This enormous long avenue of hulls that were destined to be food, gave us a sense of the vast populousness of the moon world second only to the effect of our first glimpse down the shaft.

It seemed to me at first that the Selenites must be standing on trestle-supported planks, and then I saw that the planks[1] and supports and their hatchets were really of the same leaden hue as my fetters had seemed – before white light came to bear on them.

1 I do not remember seeing any wooden things on the moon; doors, tables, everything corresponding to our terrestrial joinery was made of metal, and I believe for the most part of gold, which as a metal would, of course, naturally recommend itself – other things being equal – on account of the ease in working it, and its toughness and durability.

A number of very thick-looking crowbars lay about the floor, and had apparently assisted to turn the dead mooncalf over on its side. They were perhaps six feet long, with shaped handles, very tempting-looking weapons. The whole place was lit by three transverse streams of the blue fluid.

We lay for a long time noting all these things in silence. "Well?" said Cavor at last.

I crouched over and turned to him. I had come upon a brilliant idea. "Unless they lowered those bodies by a crane," I said, "we must be nearer the surface than I thought."

"Why?"

"The mooncalf doesn't hop, and it hasn't got wings."

He peered over the edge of the hollow again. "I wonder now..." he began. "After all, we have never gone far from the surface – "

I stopped him by a grip on his arm. I had heard a noise from the cleft below us!

We twisted ourselves about, and lay as still as death, with every sense alert. In a little while I did not doubt that something was quietly ascending the cleft. Very slowly and quite noiselessly I assured myself of a good grip on my chain, and waited for that something to appear.

"Just look at those chaps with the hatchets again," I said.

"They're all right," said Cavor.

I took a sort of provisional aim at the gap in the grating. I could hear now quite distinctly the soft twittering of the ascending Selenites, the dab of their hands against the rock, and the falling of dust from their grips as they clambered.

Then I could see that there was something moving dimly in the blackness below the grating, but what it might be I could not distinguish. The whole thing seemed to hang fire just for a moment – then smash! I had sprung to my feet, struck savagely at something that had flashed out at me. It was the keen point of a spear. I have thought since that its length in the narrowness of the cleft must have prevented its being sloped to reach me. Anyhow, it shot out from the grating like the tongue of a snake, and missed and flew back and flashed again. But the second time I snatched and caught it, and wrenched it away, but not before another had darted ineffectually at me.

I shouted with triumph as I felt the hold of the Selenite resist my pull for a moment and give, and then I was jabbing down through the bars, amidst squeals from the darkness, and Cavor had snapped off the other spear, and was leaping and flourishing it beside me, and making inefficient jabs. Clang, clang, came up through the grating, and then an axe hurtled through the air and whacked against the rocks beyond, to remind me of the fleshers at the carcasses up the cavern.

I turned, and they were all coming towards us in open order waving their axes. They were short, thick, little beggars, with long arms, strikingly different from the ones we had seen before. If they had not heard of us before, they must have realised the situation with incredible swiftness. I stared at them for a moment, spear in hand. "Guard that grating, Cavor," I cried, howled to intimidate them, and rushed to meet them. Two of them missed with their hatchets, and the rest fled incontinently. Then the two also were sprinting away up the cavern, with hands clenched and heads down. I never saw men run like them!

I knew the spear I had was no good for me. It was thin and flimsy, only effectual for a thrust, and too long for a quick recover. So I only chased the Selenites as far as the first carcass, and stopped there and picked up one of the crowbars that were lying about. It felt comfortingly heavy, and equal to smashing any number of Selenites. I threw away my spear, and picked up a second crowbar for the other hand. I felt five times better than I had with the spear. I shook the two threateningly at the Selenites, who had come to a halt in a little crowd far away up the cavern, and then turned about to look at Cavor.

He was leaping from side to side of the grating, making threatening jabs with his broken spear. That was all right. It would keep the Selenites down – for a time at any rate. I looked up the cavern again. What on earth were we going to do now?

We were cornered in a sort of way already. But these butchers up the cavern had been surprised, they were probably scared, and they had no special weapons, only those little hatchets of theirs. And that way lay escape. Their sturdy little forms – ever so much shorter and thicker than the mooncalf herds – were scattered up the slope in a way that was eloquent of indecision. I had the moral advantage of a mad bull in a street. But for all that, there seemed a tremendous crowd of them. Very probably there was. Those Selenites down the cleft had certainly some infernally long spears. It might be they had other surprises for us… But, confound it! if we charged up the cave we should let them up behind us, and if we didn't those little brutes up the cave would probably get reinforced. Heaven alone knew what tremendous engines of warfare – guns, bombs, terrestrial torpedoes – this unknown world below our feet, this vaster world of which we had only pricked the outer cuticle, might not presently send up to our destruction. It became clear the only thing to do was to charge! It became clearer as the legs of a number of fresh Selenites appeared running down the cavern towards us.

"Bedford!" cried Cavor, and behold! he was half-way between me and the grating.

"Go back!" I cried. "What are you doing – "

"They've got – it's like a gun!"

And struggling in the grating between those defensive spears appeared the head and shoulders of a singularly lean and angular Selenite, bearing some complicated apparatus.

I realised Cavor's utter incapacity for the fight we had in hand. For a moment I hesitated. Then I rushed past him whirling my crowbars, and shouting to confound the aim of the Selenite. He was aiming in the queerest way with the thing against his stomach. "*Chuzz!*" The thing wasn't a gun; it went off like cross-bow more, and dropped me in the middle of a leap.

I didn't fall down, I simply came down a little shorter than I should have done if I hadn't been hit, and from the feel of my shoulder the thing might have tapped me and glanced off. Then my left hand hit again the shaft, and I perceived there was a sort of spear sticking half through my shoulder. The moment after I got home with the crowbar in my right hand, and hit the Selenite fair and square. He collapsed – he crushed and crumpled – his head smashed like an egg.

I dropped a crowbar, pulled the spear out of my shoulder, and began to jab it down the grating into the darkness. At each jab came a shriek and twitter. Finally I hurled the spear down upon them with all my strength, leapt up, picked up the crowbar again, and started for the multitude up the cavern.

"Bedford!" cried Cavor. "Bedford!" as I flew past him.

I seem to remember his footsteps coming on behind me.

Step, leap...whack, step, leap... Each leap seemed to last ages. With each, the cave opened out and the number of Selenites visible increased. At first they seemed all running about like ants in a disturbed ant-hill, one or two waving hatchets and coming to meet me, more running away, some bolting sideways into the avenue of carcasses, then presently others came in sight carrying spears, and then others. I saw a most extraordinary thing, all hands and feet, bolting for cover. The cavern grew darker farther up. Flick! something flew over my head. Flick! As I soared in mid-stride I saw a spear hit and quiver in one of the carcasses to my left. Then, as I came down, one hit the ground before me, and I heard the remote chuzz! with which their things were fired. Flick, flick! for a moment it was a shower. They were volleying!

I stopped dead.

I don't think I thought clearly then. I seem to remember a kind of stereotyped phrase running through my mind: "Zone of fire, seek cover!" I know I made a dash for the space between two of the carcasses, and stood there panting and feeling very wicked.

I looked round for Cavor, and for a moment it seemed as if he had vanished from the world. Then he came out of the darkness between the row of the carcasses and the rocky wall of the cavern. I saw his little face, dark and blue, and shining with perspiration and emotion.

He was saying something, but what it was I did not heed. I had realised that we might work from mooncalf to mooncalf up the cave until we were near enough to charge home. It was charge or nothing. "Come on!" I said, and led the way.

"Bedford!" he cried unavailingly.

My mind was busy as we went up that narrow alley between the dead bodies and the wall of the cavern. The rocks curved about – they could not enfilade us. Though in that narrow space we could not leap, yet with our earth-born strength we were still able to go very much faster than the Selenites. I reckoned we should presently come right among them. Once we were on them, they would be nearly as formidable as black beetles. Only! – there would first of all be a volley. I thought of a stratagem. I whipped off my flannel jacket as I ran.

"Bedford!" panted Cavor behind me.

I glanced back. "What?" said I.

He was pointing upward over the carcasses. "White light!" he said. "White light again!"

I looked, and it was even so, a faint white ghost of light in the remoter cavern roof. That seemed to give me double strength.

"Keep close," I said. A flat, long Selenite dashed out of the darkness, and squealed and fled. I halted, and stopped Cavor with my hand. I hung my jacket over my crowbar, ducked round the next carcass, dropped jacket and crowbar, showed myself, and darted back.

"Chuzz – flick," just one arrow came. We were close on the Selenites, and they were standing in a crowd, broad, short, and tall together, with a little battery of their shooting implements pointing down the cave. Three or four other arrows followed the first, then their fire ceased.

I stuck out my head, and escaped by a hair's-breadth. This time I drew a dozen shots or more, and heard the Selenites shouting and twittering as if with excitement as they shot. I picked up jacket and crowbar again.

"*Now!*" said I, and thrust out the jacket.

"Chuzz-zz-zz-zz! Chuzz!" In an instant my jacket had grown a thick beard of arrows, and they were quivering all over the carcass behind us. Instantly I slipped the crowbar out of the jacket,

154

dropped the jacket – for all I know to the contrary it is lying up there in the moon now – and rushed out upon them.

For a minute perhaps it was massacre. I was too fierce to discriminate, and the Selenites were probably too scared to fight. At any rate they made no sort of fight against me. I saw scarlet, as the saying is. I remember I seemed to be wading among those leathery, thin things as a man wades through tall grass, mowing and hitting, first right, then left; smash. Little drops of moisture flew about. I trod on things that crushed and piped and went slippery. The crowd seemed to open and close and flow like water. They seemed to have no combined plan whatever. There were spears flew about me, I was grazed over the ear by one. I was stabbed once in the arm and once in the cheek, but I only found that out afterwards, when the blood had had time to run and cool and feel wet.

What Cavor did I do not know. For a space it seemed that this fighting had lasted for an age, and must needs go on for ever. Then suddenly it was all over, and there was nothing to be seen but the backs of heads bobbing up and down as their owners ran in all directions... I seemed altogether unhurt. I ran forward some paces, shouting, then turned about. I was amazed.

I had come right through them in vast flying strides, they were all behind me, and running hither and thither to hide.

I felt an enormous astonishment at the evaporation of the great fight into which I had hurled myself, and not a little exultation. It did not seem to me that I had discovered the Selenites were unexpectedly flimsy, but that I was unexpectedly strong. I laughed stupidly. This fantastic moon!

I glanced for a moment at the smashed and writhing bodies that were scattered over the cavern floor, with a vague idea of further violence, then hurried on after Cavor.

# CHAPTER EIGHTEEN

## In the Sunlight

P resently we saw that the cavern before us opened on a hazy void. In another moment we had emerged upon a sort of slanting gallery, that projected into a vast circular space, a huge cylindrical pit running vertically up and down. Round this pit the slanting gallery ran without any parapet or protection for a turn and a half, and then plunged high above into the rock again. Somehow it reminded me then of one of those spiral turns of the railway through the Saint Gothard. It was all tremendously huge. I can scarcely hope to convey to you the Titanic proportion of all that place, the Titanic effect of it. Our eyes followed up the vast declivity of the pit wall, and overhead and far above we beheld a round opening set with faint stars, and half of the lip about it well nigh blinding with the white light of the sun. At that we cried aloud simultaneously.

"Come on!" I said, leading the way.

"But there?" said Cavor, and very carefully stepped nearer the edge of the gallery. I followed his example, and craned forward and looked down, but I was dazzled by that gleam of light above, and I could see only a bottomless darkness with spectral patches of crimson and purple floating therein. Yet if I could not see, I could hear. Out of this darkness came a sound, a sound like the angry hum one can hear if one puts one's ear outside a hive of bees, a sound out of that enormous hollow, it may be, four miles beneath our feet...

For a moment I listened, then tightened my grip on my crowbar, and led the way up the gallery.

"This must be the shaft we looked down upon," said Cavor. "Under that lid."

"And below there, is where we saw the lights."

"The lights!" said he. "Yes – the lights of the world that now we shall never see."

"We'll come back," I said, for now we had escaped so much I was rashly sanguine that we should recover the sphere.

His answer I did not catch.

"Eh?" I asked.

"It doesn't matter," he answered, and we hurried on in silence.

I suppose that slanting lateral way was four or five miles long, allowing for its curvature, and it ascended at a slope that would have made it almost impossibly steep on earth, but which one strode up easily under lunar conditions. We saw only two Selenites during all that portion of our flight, and directly they became aware of us they ran headlong. It was clear that the knowledge of our strength and violence had reached them. Our way to the exterior was unexpectedly plain. The spiral gallery straightened into a steeply ascendent tunnel, its floor bearing abundant traces of the mooncalves, and so straight and short in proportion to its vast arch, that no part of it was absolutely dark. Almost immediately it began to lighten, and then far off and high up, and quite blindingly brilliant, appeared its opening on the exterior, a slope of Alpine steepness surmounted by a crest of bayonet shrub, tall and broken down now, and dry and dead, in spiky silhouette against the sun.

And it is strange that we men, to whom this very vegetation had seemed so weird and horrible a little time ago, should now behold it with the emotion a home-coming exile might feel at sight of his native land. We welcomed even the rareness of the air that made us pant as we ran, and which rendered speaking no longer the easy thing that it had been, but an effort to make oneself heard. Larger grew the sunlit circle above us, and larger, and all the nearer tunnel sank into a rim of indistinguishable black. We saw the dead bayonet shrub no longer with any touch of green in it, but brown and dry and thick, and the shadow of its upper branches high out of sight made a densely interlaced pattern upon the tumbled rocks. And at the immediate mouth of the tunnel was a wide trampled space where the mooncalves had come and gone.

We came out upon this space at last into a light and heat that hit and pressed upon us. We traversed the exposed area painfully, and clambered up a slope among the scrub stems, and sat down at last panting in a high place beneath the shadow of a mass of twisted lava. Even in the shade the rock felt hot.

The air was intensely hot, and we were in great physical discomfort, but for all that we were no longer in a nightmare. We seemed to have come to our own province again, beneath the stars. All the fear and stress of our flight through the dim passages and fissures below had fallen from us. That last fight had filled us with an enormous confidence in ourselves so far as the Selenites were concerned. We looked back almost incredulously at the black opening from which we had just emerged. Down there it was, in a blue glow that now in our memories seemed the next thing to absolute darkness, we had met with things like mad mockeries of men, helmet-headed creatures, and had walked in fear before them, and had submitted to them until we could submit no longer. And behold, they had smashed like wax and scattered like chaff, and fled and vanished like the creatures of a dream!

I rubbed my eyes, doubting whether we had not slept and dreamt these things by reason of the fungus we had eaten, and suddenly discovered the blood upon my face, and then that my shirt was sticking painfully to my shoulder and arm.

"Confound it!" I said, gauging my injuries with an investigatory hand, and suddenly that distant tunnel mouth became, as it were, a watching eye.

"Cavor!" I said; "what are they going to do now? And what are we going to do?"

He shook his head, with his eyes fixed upon the tunnel. "How can one tell what they will do?"

"It depends on what they think of us, and I don't see how we can begin to guess that. And it depends upon what they have in reserve. It's as you say, Cavor, we have touched the merest outside of this world. They may have all sorts of things inside here. Even with those shooting things they might make it bad for us…

"Yet after all," I said, "even if we *don't* find the sphere at once, there is a chance for us. We might hold out. Even through the night. We might go down there again and make a fight for it."

I stared about me with speculative eyes. The character of the scenery had altered altogether by reason of the enormous growth and subsequent drying of the scrub. The crest on which we sat was high, and commanded a wide prospect of the crater landscape, and we saw it now all sere and dry in the late autumn of the lunar afternoon. Rising one behind the other were long slopes and fields of trampled brown where the mooncalves had pastured, and far away in the full blaze of the sun a drove of them basked slumberously, scattered shapes, each with a blot of shadow against it like sheep on the side of a down. But never a sign of a Selenite was to be seen. Whether they had fled on our emergence from the interior passages, or whether they were accustomed to retire after driving out the mooncalves, I cannot guess. At the time I believed the former was the case.

"If we were to set fire to all this stuff, I said, "we might find the sphere among the ashes."

Cavor did not seem to hear me. He was peering under his hand at the stars, that still, in spite of the intense sunlight, were abundantly visible in the sky. "How long do you think we've have been here?" he asked at last.

"Been where?"

"On the moon."

"Two earthly days, perhaps."

"More nearly ten. Do you know, the sun is past its zenith, and sinking in the west. In four days' time or less it will be night."

"But – we've only eaten once!"

"I know that. And – But there are the stars!"

"But why should time seem different because we are on a smaller planet?"

"I don't know. There it is!"

"How does one tell time?"

"Hunger – fatigue – all those things are different. Everything is different – everything. To me it seems that since first we came

161

out of the sphere has been only a question of hours – long hours
– at most."

"Ten days," I said; "that leaves – " I looked up at the sun for
a moment, and then saw that it was halfway from the zenith to
the western edge of things. "Four days!... Cavor, we musn't sit
here and dream. How do you think we may begin?"

I stood up. "We must get a fixed point we can recognise – we
might hoist a flag, or a handkerchief, or something – and quarter
the ground, and work round that."

He stood up beside me.

"Yes," he said, "there is nothing for it but to hunt the sphere.
Nothing. We may find it – certainly we may find it. And if not – "

"We must keep on looking."

He looked this way and that, glanced up at the sky and down
at the tunnel, and astonished me by a sudden gesture of
impatience. "Oh! but we have done foolishly! To have come to
this pass! Think how it might have been, and the things we might
have done!"

"We might do something yet."

"Never the thing we might have done. Here below our feet is
a world. Think of what that world must be! Think of that
machine we saw, and the lid and the shaft! They were just remote
outlying things, and those creatures we have seen and fought
with no more than ignorant peasants, dwellers in the outskirts,
yokels and labourers half akin to brutes. Down below! Caverns
beneath caverns, tunnels, structures, ways... It must open out,
and be greater and wider and more populous as one descends.
Assuredly. Right down at the last to the central sea that washes
round the core of the moon. Think of its inky waters under
the spare lights – if, indeed, their eyes *need* lights! Think of the

162

cascading tributaries pouring down their channels to feed it! Think of the tides upon its surface, and the rush and swirl of its ebb and flow! Perhaps they have ships that go upon it, perhaps down there are mighty cities and swarming ways, and wisdom and order passing the wit of man. And we may die here upon it, and never see the masters who *must* be – ruling over these things! We may freeze and die here, and the air will freeze and thaw upon us, and then – ! Then they will come upon us, come on our stiff and silent bodies, and find the sphere we cannot find, and they will understand at last too late all the thought and effort that ended here in vain!"

His voice for all that speech sounded like the voice of someone heard in a telephone, weak and far away.

"But the darkness," I said.

"One might get over that."

"How?"

"I don't know. How am I to know? One might carry a torch, one might have a lamp – The others – might understand."

He stood for a moment with his hands held down and a rueful face, staring out over the waste that defied him. Then with a gesture of renunciation he turned towards me with proposals for the systematic hunting of the sphere.

"We can return," I said.

He looked about him. "First of all we shall have to get to earth."

"We could bring back lamps to carry and climbing irons, and a hundred necessary things."

"Yes," he said.

"We can take back an earnest of success in this gold."

He looked at my golden crowbars, and said nothing for a space. He stood with his hands clasped behind his back, staring across the crater. At last he sighed and spoke. "It was *I* found the way here, but to find a way isn't always to be master of a way. If I take my secret back to earth, what will happen? I do not see how I can keep my secret for a year, for even a part of a year. Sooner or later it must come out, even if other men rediscover it. And then... Governments and powers will struggle to get hither, they will fight against one another, and against these moon people; it will only spread warfare and multiply the occasions of war. In a little while, in a very little while, if I tell my secret, this planet to its deepest galleries will be strewn with human dead. Other things are doubtful, but that is certain... It is not as though man had any use for the moon. What good would the moon be to men? Even of their own planet what have they made but a battle-ground and theatre of infinite folly? Small as his world is, and short as his time, he has still in his little life down there far more than he can do. No! Science has toiled too long forging weapons for fools to use. It is time she held her hand. Let him find it out for himself again – in a thousand years' time."

"There are methods of secrecy," I said.

He looked up at me and smiled. "After all," he said, "why should one worry? There is little chance of our finding the sphere, and down below things are brewing. It's simply the human habit of hoping till we die that makes us think of return. Our troubles are only beginning. We have shown these moon folk violence, we have given them a taste of our quality, and our chances are about as good as a tiger's that has got loose and killed a man in Hyde Park. The news of us must be running down from gallery to gallery, down towards the central parts... No sane beings will ever let us take that sphere back to earth after so much as they have seen of us."

"We aren't improving our chances," said I, "by sitting here."

We stood up side by side.

"After all," he said, "we must separate. We must stick up a handkerchief on these tall spikes here and fasten it firmly, and from this as a centre we must work over the crater. You must go westward, moving out in semicircles to and fro towards the setting sun. You must move first with your shadow on your right until it is at right angles with the direction of your handkerchief, and then with your shadow on your left. And I will do the same to the east. We will look into every gully, examine every skerry of rocks; we will do all we can to find my sphere. If we see the Selenites we will hide from them as well as we can. For drink we must take snow, and if we feel the need of food, we must kill a mooncalf if we can, and eat such flesh as it has – raw – and so each will go his own way."

"And if one of us comes upon the sphere?"

"He must come back to the white handkerchief, and stand by it and signal to the other."

"And if neither – ?"

Cavor glanced up at the sun. "We go on seeking until the night and cold overtake us."

"Suppose the Selenites have found the sphere and hidden it?"

He shrugged his shoulders.

"Or if presently they come hunting us?"

He made no answer.

"You had better take a club," I said.

He shook his head, and stared away from me across the waste.

But for a moment he did not start. He looked round at me shyly, hesitated. "*Au revoir,*" he said.

I felt an odd stab of emotion. A sense of how we had galled each other, and particularly how I must have galled him, came to me. "Confound it," thought I, "we might have done better!" I was on the point of asking him to shake hands – for that, somehow, was how I felt just then – when he put his feet together and leapt away from me towards the north. He seemed to drift through the air as a dead leaf would do, fell lightly, and leapt again. I stood for a moment watching him, then faced westward reluctantly, pulled myself together, and with something of the feeling of a man who leaps into icy water, selected a leaping point, and plunged forward to explore my solitary half of the moon world. I dropped rather clumsily among rocks, stood up and looked about me, clambered on to a rocky slab, and leapt again...

When presently I looked for Cavor he was hidden from my eyes, but the handkerchief showed out bravely on its headland, white in the blaze of the sun.

I determined not to lose sight of that handkerchief whatever might betide.

# CHAPTER NINETEEN

## Mr Bedford Alone

In a little while it seemed to me as though I had always been alone on the moon. I hunted for a time with a certain intentness, but the heat was still very great, and the thinness of the air felt like a hoop about one's chest. I came presently into a hollow basin bristling with tall, brown, dry fronds about its edge, and I sat down under these to rest and cool. I intended to rest for only a little while. I put down my clubs beside me, and sat resting my chin on my hands. I saw with a sort of colourless interest that the rocks of the basin, where here and there the crackling dry lichens had shrunk away to show them, were all veined and splattered with gold, that here and there bosses of rounded and wrinkled gold projected from among the litter. What did that matter now? A sort of languor had possession of my limbs and mind, I did not belive for a moment that we should ever find the sphere in that vast desiccated wilderness. I seemed to lack a motive for effort until the Selenites should come. Then I supposed I should exert myself, obeying that unreasonable imperative that urges a man before all things to preserve and defend his life, albeit he may preserve it only to die more painfully in a little while.

Why had we come to the moon?

The thing presented itself to me as a perplexing problem. What is this spirit in man that urges him for ever to depart from happiness and security, to toil, to place himself in danger, to risk even a reasonable certainty of death? It dawned upon me up there in the moon as a thing I ought always to have known, that man is not made simply to go about being safe and comfortable and well fed and amused. Almost any man, if you put the thing to him, not in words, but in the shape of opportunities, will show that he knows as much. Against his interest, against his happiness, he is constantly being driven to do unreasonable things. Some force not himself impels him, and go he must. But why? Why? Sitting there in the midst of that useless moon gold, amidst the things of another world, I took count of all my life. Assuming I was to die a castaway upon the moon, I failed altogether to see what purpose I had served. I got no light on that point, but at any rate it was clearer to me than it had ever been in my life before that I was not serving my own purpose, that all my life I had in truth never served the purposes of my private life. Whose purposes, what purposes, was I serving?... I ceased to speculate on why we had come to the moon, and took a wider sweep. Why had I come to the earth? Why had I a private life at all?... I lost myself at last in bottomless speculations...

My thoughts became vague and cloudy, no longer leading in definite directions. I had not felt heavy or weary – I cannot imagine one doing so upon the moon – but I suppose I was greatly fatigued. At any rate I slept.

Slumbering there rested me greatly, I think, and the sun was setting and the violence of the heat abating, through all the time I slumbered. When at last I was roused from my slumbers by a remote clamour, I felt active and capable again. I rubbed my eyes and stretched my arms. I rose to my feet – I was a little stiff – and at once prepared to resume my search. I shouldered my golden clubs, one on each shoulder, and went on out of the ravine of the gold-veined rocks.

The sun was certainly lower, much lower than it had been; the air was very much cooler. I perceived I must have slept some time. It seemed to me that a faint touch of misty blueness hung about the western cliff. I leapt to a little boss of rock and surveyed the crater. I could see no signs of mooncalves or Selenites, nor could I see Cavor, but I could see my handkerchief afar off, spread out on its thicket of thorns. I looked about me, and then leapt forward to the next convenient view-point.

I beat my round in a semicircle, and back again in a still remoter crescent. It was very fatiguing and hopeless. The air was really very much cooler, and it seemed to me that the shadow under the westward cliff was growing broad. Ever and again I stopped and reconnoitred, but there was no sign of Cavor, no sign of Selenites; and it seemed to me the mooncalves must have been driven into the interior again – I could see none of them. I became more and more desirous of seeing Cavor. The winged outline of the sun had sunk now, until it was scarcely the distance of its diameter from the rim of the sky. I was oppressed by the idea that the Selenites would presently close their lids and valves, and shut us out under the inexorable onrush of the lunar night. It seemed to me high time that he abandoned his search, and that we took counsel together. I felt how urgent it was that we should decide soon upon our course. We had failed to find the sphere, we no longer had time to seek it, and once these valves were closed with us outside, we were lost men. The great night of space would descend upon us – that blackness of the void which is the only absolute death. All my being shrank from that approach. We must get into the moon again, though we were slain in doing it. I was haunted by a vision of our freezing to death, of our hammering with our last strength on the valve of the great pit.

I took no thought any more of the sphere. I thought only of finding Cavor again. I was half inclined to go back into the moon without him, rather than seek him until it was too late. I was already half-way back towards our handkerchief, when suddenly –

I saw the sphere!

I did not find it so much as it found me. It was lying much farther to the westward than I had gone, and the sloping rays of the sinking sun reflected from its glass had suddenly proclaimed its presence in a dazzling beam. For an instant I thought this was some new device of the Selenites against us, and then I understood.

I threw up my arms, shouted a ghostly shout, and set off in vast leaps towards it. I missed one of my leaps and dropped into a deep ravine and twisted my ankle, and after that I stumbled at almost every leap. I was in a state of hysterical agitation, trembling violently, and quite breathless long before I got to it. Three times at least I had to stop with my hands resting on my side and spite of the thin dryness of the air, the perspiration was wet upon my face.

I thought of nothing but the sphere until I reached it, I forgot even my trouble of Cavor's whereabouts. My last leap flung me with my hands hard against its glass; then I lay against it panting, and trying vainly to shout, "Cavor! here is the sphere!" When I had recovered a little I peered through the thick glass, and the things inside seemed tumbled. I stooped to peer closer. Then I attempted to get in. I had to hoist it over a little to get my head through the manhole. The screw stopper was inside, and I could see now that nothing had been touched, nothing had suffered. It lay there as we had left it when we had dropped out amidst the snow. For a time I was wholly occupied in making and remaking this inventory. I found I was trembling violently. It was good to see that familiar dark interior again! I cannot tell you how good. Presently I crept inside and sat down among the things. I looked through the glass at the moon world and shivered. I placed my gold clubs upon the table, and sought out and took a little food; not so much because I wanted it, but because it was there. Then it occurred to me that it was time to go out and signal for Cavor. But I did not go out and signal for Cavor forthwith. Something held me to the sphere.

After all, everything was coming right. There would be still time for us to get more of the magic stone that gives one mastery over men. Away there, close handy, was gold for the picking up; and the sphere would travel as well half full of gold as though it were empty. We could go back now, masters of ourselves and our world, and then –

I roused myself at last, and with an effort got myself out of the sphere. I shivered as I emerged, for the evening air was growing very cold. I stood in the hollow staring about me. I scrutinised the bushes round me very carefully before I leapt to the rocky shelf hard by, and took once more what had been my first leap in the moon. But now I made it with no effort whatever.

The growth and decay of the vegetation had gone on apace, and the whole aspect of the rocks had changed, but still it was possible to make out the slope on which the seeds had germinated, and the rocky mass from which we had taken our first view of the crater. But the spiky shrub on the slope stood brown and sere now, and thirty feet high, and cast long shadows that stretched out of sight, and the little seeds that clustered in its upper branches were brown and ripe. Its work was done, and it was brittle and ready to fall and crumple under the freezing air, so soon as the nightfall came. And the huge cacti, that had swollen as we watched them, had long since burst and scattered their spores to the four quarters of the moon. Amazing little corner in the universe – the landing-place of men!

Some day, thought I, I will have an inscription standing there right in the midst of the hollow. It came to me, if only this teeming world within knew of the full import of the moment, how furious its tumult would become!

But as yet it could scarcely be dreaming of the significance of our coming. For if it did, the crater would surely be an uproar of pursuit, instead of as still as death! I looked about for some place from which I might signal Cavor, and saw that same patch of rock to which he had leapt from my present standpoint, still bare and barren in the sun. For a moment I hesitated at going so far from the sphere. Then with a pang of shame at that hesitation, I leapt...

From this vantage point I surveyed the crater again. Far away at the top of the enormous shadow I cast was the little white handkerchief fluttering on the bushes. It was very little and very far, and Cavor was not in sight. It seemed to me that by this time he ought to be looking for me. That was the agreement. But he was nowhere to be seen.

I stood waiting and watching, hands shading my eyes, expecting every moment to distinguish him. Very probably I stood there for quite a long time. I tried to shout, and was reminded of the thinness of the air. I made an undecided step back towards the sphere. But a lurking dread of the Selenites made me hesitate to signal my whereabouts by hoisting one of our sleeping-blankets onto the adjacent scrub. I searched the crater again.

It had an effect of emptiness that chilled me. And it was still; any sound from the Selenites in the world beneath, even had died away. It was as still as death. Save for the faint stir of the shrub about me in the little breeze that was rising, there was no sound nor shadow of a sound. And the breeze blew chill.

Confound Cavor!

I took a deep breath. I put my hands to the sides of my mouth. "Cavor!" I bawled, and the sound was like some manikin shouting far away.

I looked at the handkerchief, I looked behind me at the broadening shadow of the westward cliff, I looked under my hand at the sun. It seemed to me that almost visibly it was creeping down the sky.

I felt I must act instantly if I was to save Cavor. I whipped off my vest and flung it as a mark on the sere bayonets of the shrubs behind me, and then set off in a straight line towards the handkerchief. Perhaps it was a couple of miles away – a matter of a few hundred leaps and strides. I have already told how one seemed to hang through those lunar leaps. In each suspense I sought Cavor, and marvelled why he should be hidden. In each leap I could feel the sun setting behind me. Each time I touched the ground I was tempted to go back.

A last leap and I was in the depression below our handkerchief, a stride, and I stood on our former vantage point within arms' reach of it. I stood up straight and scanned the world about me, between its lengthening bars of shadow. Far away, down a long declivity, was the opening of the tunnel up which we had fled, and my shadow reached towards it, stretched towards it, and touched it, like a finger of the night.

Not a sign of Cavor, not a sound in all the stillness, only the stir and waving of the scrub and of the shadows increased. And suddenly and violently I shivered. "Cav – " I began, and realised once more the uselessness of the human voice in that thin air.

Silence. The silence of death.

Then it was my eye caught something – a little thing lying, perhaps fifty yards away down the slope, amidst a litter of bent and broken branches. What was it? I knew, and yet for some reason I would not know.

I went nearer to it. It was the little cricket-cap Cavor had worn. I did not touch it, I stood looking at it.

I saw then that the scattered branches about it had been forcibly smashed and trampled. I hesitated, stepped forward, and picked it up.

I stood with Cavor's cap in my hand, staring at the trampled reeds and thorns about me. On some of them were little smears of something dark, something that I dared not touch. A dozen yards away, perhaps, the rising breeze dragged something into view, something small and vividly white.

It was a little piece of paper crumpled tightly, as though it had been clutched tightly. I picked it up, and on it were smears of red. My eye caught faint pencil marks. I smoothed it out, and saw uneven and broken writing ending at last in a crooked streak upon the paper.

I set myself to decipher this.

"I have been injured about the knee, I think my kneecap is hurt, and I cannot run or crawl," it began – pretty distinctly written.

Then less legibly: "They have been chasing me for some time, and it is only a question of" – the word "time" seemed to have been written here and erased in favour of something illegible – "before they get me. They are beating all about me."

Then the writing became convulsive. "I can hear them," I guessed the tracing meant, and then it was quite unreadable for a space. Then came a little string of words that were quite distinct: "a different sort of Selenite altogether, who appears to be directing the – " The writing became a mere hasty confusion again.

"They have larger brain cases – much larger, and slenderer bodies, and very short legs. They make gentle noises, and move with organized deliberation...

"And though I am wounded and helpless here, their appearance still gives me hope – " That was like Cavor. "They have not shot at me or attempted...injury. I intend – "

Then came the sudden streak of the pencil across the paper, and on the back and edges – blood!

And as I stood there stupid, and perplexed, with this dumbfounding relic in my hand, something very soft and light and chill touched my hand for a moment and ceased to be, and then a thing, a little white speck, drifted athwart a shadow. It was a tiny snowflake, the first snowflake, the herald of the night.

I looked up with a start, and the sky had darkened almost to blackness, and was thick with a gathering multitude of coldly watchful stars. I looked eastward, and the light of that shrivelled world was touched with sombre bronze; westward, and the sun

175

robbed now by a thickening white mist of half its heat and splendour, was touching the crater rim, was sinking out of sight, and all the shrubs and jagged and tumbled rocks stood out against it in a bristling disorder of black shapes. Into the great lake of darkness westward, a vast wreath of mist was sinking. A cold wind set all the crater shivering. Suddenly, for a moment, I was in a puff of falling snow, and all the world about me gray and dim.

And then it was I heard, not loud and penetrating as at first, but faint and dim like a dying voice, that tolling, that same tolling that had welcomed the coming of the day: Boom!... Boom!... Boom!...

It echoed about the crater, it seemed to throb with the throbbing of the greater stars, the blood-red crescent of the sun's disc sank as it tolled out: Boom!... Boom!... Boom!...

What had happened to Cavor? All through that tolling I stood there stupidly, and at last the tolling ceased.

And suddenly the open mouth of the tunnel down below there, shut like an eye and vanished out of sight.

Then indeed was I alone.

Over me, around me, closing in on me, embracing me ever nearer, was the Eternal; that which was before the beginning, and that which triumphs over the end; that enormous void in which all light and life and being is but the thin and vanishing splendour of a falling star, the cold, the stillness, the silence – the infinite and final Night of space.

The sense of solitude and desolation became the sense of an overwhelming presence that stooped towards me, that almost touched me.

176

"No," I cried. "*No!* Not yet! not yet! Wait! Wait! Oh, wait!" My voice went up to a shriek. I flung the crumpled paper from me, scrambled back to the crest to take my bearings, and then, with all the will that was in me, leapt out towards the mark I had left, dim and distant now in the very margin of the shadow.

Leap, leap, leap, and each leap was seven ages.

Before me the pale serpent-girdled section of the sun sank and sank, and the advancing shadow swept to seize the sphere before I could reach it. I was two miles away, a hundred leaps or more, and the air about me was thinning out as it thins under an air-pump, and the cold was gripping at my joints. But had I died, I should have died leaping. Once, and then again my foot slipped on the gathering snow as I leapt and shortened my leap; once I fell short into bushes that crashed and smashed into dusty chips and nothingness, and once I stumbled as I dropped and rolled head over heels into a gully, and rose bruised and bleeding and confused as to my direction.

But such incidents were as nothing to the intervals, those awful pauses when one drifted through the air towards that pouring tide of night. My breathing made a piping noise, and it was as though knives were whirling in my lungs. My heart seemed to beat against the top of my brain. "Shall I reach it? O Heaven! Shall I reach it?"

My whole being became anguish.

"Lie down!" screamed my pain and despair; "lie down!"

The nearer I struggled, the more awfully remote it seemed. I was numb, I stumbled, I bruised and cut myself and did not bleed.

It was in sight.

I fell on all fours, and my lungs whooped.

I crawled. The frost gathered on my lips, icicles hung from my moustache, I was white with the freezing atmosphere.

I was a dozen yards from it. My eyes had become dim. "Lie down!" screamed despair; "lie down!"

I touched it, and halted. "Too late!" screamed despair; "lie down!"

I fought stiffly with it. I was on the manhole lip, a stupefied, half-dead being. The snow was all about me. I pulled myself in. There lurked within a little warmer air.

The snowflakes – the airflakes – danced in about me, as I tried with chilling hands to thrust the valve in and spun it tight and hard. I sobbed. "I will," I chattered in my teeth. And then, with fingers that quivered and felt brittle, I turned to the shutter studs.

As I fumbled with the switches – for I had never controlled them before – I could see dimly through the steaming glass the blazing red streamers of the sinking sun, dancing and flickering through the snowstorm, and the black forms of the scrub thickening and bending and breaking beneath the accumulating snow. Thicker whirled the snow and thicker, black against the light. What if even now the switches overcame me?

Then something clicked under my hands, and in an instant that last vision of the moon world was hidden from my eyes. I was in the silence and darkness of the inter-planetary sphere.

# CHAPTER TWENTY

## Mr Bedford in Infinite Space

It was almost as though I had been killed. Indeed, I could imagine a man suddenly and violently killed would feel very much as I did. One moment, a passion of agonising existence and fear; the next darkness and stillness, neither light nor life nor sun, moon nor stars, the blank infinite. Although the thing was done by my own act, although I had already tasted this very effect in Cavor's company, I felt astonished, dumbfounded, and overwhelmed. I seemed to be borne upward into an enormous darkness. My fingers floated off the studs, I hung as if I were annihilated, and at last very softly and gently I came against the bale and the golden chain, and the crowbars that had drifted to the middle of the sphere.

I do not know how long that drifting took. In the sphere of course, even more than on the moon, one's earthly time sense was ineffectual. At the touch of the bale it was as if I had awakened from a dreamless sleep. I immediately perceived that if I wanted to keep awake and alive I must get a light or open a window, so as to get a grip of something with my eyes. And besides, I was cold. I kicked off from the bale, therefore, clawed on to the thin cords within the glass, crawled along until I got to the manhole rim, and so got my bearings for the light and blind studs, took a shove off, and flying once round the bale, and getting a scare from something big and flimsy that was drifting loose, I got my hand on the cord quite close to the studs, and reached them. I lit the little lamp first of all to see what it was I had collided with, and discovered that old copy of *Lloyd's News* had slipped its moorings, and was adrift in the void. That brought me out of the infinite to my own proper dimensions again. It made me laugh and pant for a time, and suggested the idea of a little oxygen from one of the cylinders. After that I lit the heater until I felt warm, and then I took food. Then I set to work in a very gingerly fashion on the Cavorite blinds, to see if I could guess by any means how the sphere was travelling.

The first blind I opened I shut at once, and hung for a time flattened and blinded by the sunlight that had hit me. After thinking a little I started upon the windows at right angles to this one, and got the huge crescent moon and the little crescent earth behind it, the second time. I was amazed to find how far I was from the moon. I had reckoned that not only should I have little or none of the "kick-off" that the earth's atmosphere had given us at our start, but that the tangential "fly off" of the moon's spin would be at least twenty-eight times less than the earth's. I had expected to discover myself hanging over our crater, and on the edge of the night, but all that was now only a part of the outline of the white crescent that filled the sky. And Cavor – ?

He was already infinite.

I tried to imagine what could have happened to him. But at that time I could think of nothing but death. I seemed to see him, bent and smashed at the foot of some interminably high cascade of blue. And all about him the stupid insects stared...

Under the inspiring touch of the drifting newspaper I became practical again for a while. It was quite clear to me that what I had to do was to get back to earth, but as far as I could see I was drifting away from it. Whatever had happened to Cavor, even if he was still alive, which seemed to me incredible after that blood-stained scrap, I was powerless to help him. There he was, living or dead behind the mantle of that rayless night, and there he must remain at least until I could summon our fellow men to his assistance. Should I do that? Something of the sort I had in my mind; to come back to earth if it were possible, and then as maturer consideration might determine, either to show and explain the sphere to a few discreet persons, and act with them, or else to keep my secret, sell my gold, obtain weapons, provisions, and an assistant, and return with these advantages to deal on equal terms with the flimsy people of the moon, to rescue Cavor, if that were still possible, and at any rate to procure a sufficient supply of gold to place my subsequent proceedings on a firmer basis. But that was hoping far; I had first to get back.

I set myself to decide just exactly how the return to earth could be contrived. As I struggled with that problem I ceased to worry about what I should do when I got there. At last my only care was to get back.

I puzzled out at last that my best chance would be to drop back towards the moon as near as I dared in order to gather velocity, then to shut my windows, and fly behind it, and when I was past to open my earthward windows, and so get off at a good pace homeward. But whether I should ever reach the earth by that device, or whether I might not simply find myself spinning about it in some hyperbolic or parabolic curve or other, I could not tell. Later I had a happy inspiration, and by opening certain windows to the moon, which had appeared in the sky in front of the earth, I turned my course aside so as to head off the earth, which it had become evident to me I must pass behind without some such expedient. I did a very great deal of complicated thinking over these, problems – for I am no mathematician – and in the end I am certain it was much more my good luck than my reasoning that enabled me to hit the earth. Had I known then, as I know now, the mathematical chances there were against me, I doubt if I should have troubled even to touch the studs to make any attempt. And having puzzled out what I considered to be the thing to do, I opened all my moonward windows, and squatted down – the effort lifted me for a time some feet or so into the air, and I hung there in the oddest way – and waited for the crescent to get bigger and bigger until I felt I was near enough for safety. Then I would shut the windows, fly past the moon with the velocity I had got from it – if I did not smash upon it – and so go on towards the earth.

And that is what I did.

At last I felt my moonward start was sufficient. I shut out the sight of the moon from my eyes, and in a state of mind that was, I now recall, incredibly free from anxiety or any distressful quality, I sat down to begin a vigil in that little speck of matter in infinite space that would last until I should strike the earth. The heater had made the sphere tolerably warm, the air had been refreshed by the oxygen, and except for that faint congestion of the head that was always with me while I was away from earth, I felt entire physical comfort. I had extinguished the light again, lest it should fail me in the end; I was in darkness, save for the earthshine and the glitter of the stars below me. Everything was so absolutely silent and still that I might indeed have been the only being in the universe, and yet, strangely enough, I had no more feeling of loneliness or fear than if I had been lying in bed on earth. Now, this seems all the stranger to me, since during my last hours in that crater of the moon, the sense of my utter loneliness had been an agony…

Incredible as it will seem, this interval of time that I spent in space has no sort of proportion to any other interval of time in my life. Sometimes it seemed as though I sat through immeasurable eternities like some god upon a lotus leaf, and again as though there was a momentary pause as I leapt from moon to earth. In truth, it was altogether some weeks of earthly time. But I had done with care and anxiety, hunger or fear, for that space. I floated, thinking with a strange breadth and freedom of all that we had undergone, and of all my life and motives, and the secret issues of my being. I seemed to myself to have grown greater and greater, to have lost all sense of movement; to be floating amidst the stars, and always the sense of earth's littleness and the infinite littleness of my life upon it, was implicit in my thoughts.

I can't profess to explain the things that happened in my mind. No doubt they could all be traced directly or indirectly to the curious physical conditions under which I was living. I set them down here just for what they are worth, and without any comment. The most prominent quality of it was a pervading doubt of my own identity. I became, if I may so express it, dissociate from Bedford; I looked down on Bedford as a trivial, incidental thing with which I chanced to be connected. I saw Bedford in many relations – as an ass or as a poor beast, where I had hitherto been inclined to regard him with a quiet pride as a very spirited or rather forcible person. I saw him not only as an ass, but as the son of many generations of asses. I reviewed his schooldays and his early manhood, and his first encounter with love, very much as one might review the proceedings of an ant in the sand... Something of that period of lucidity I regret still hangs about me, and I doubt if I shall ever recover the full-bodied self-satisfaction of my early days. But at the time the thing was not in the least painful, because I had that extraordinary persuasion that, as a matter of fact, I was no more Bedford than I was anyone else, but only a mind floating in the still serenity of space. Why should I be disturbed about this Bedford's shortcomings? I was not responsible for him or them.

For a time I struggled against this really very grotesque delusion. I tried to summon the memory of vivid moments, of tender or intense emotions to my assistance; I felt that if I could recall one genuine twinge of feeling the growing severance would be stopped. But I could not do it. I saw Bedford rushing down Chancery Lane, hat on the back of his head, coat tails flying out, *en route* for his public examination. I saw him dodging and bumping against, and even saluting, other similar little creatures in that swarming gutter of people. Me? I saw Bedford that same evening in the sitting-room of a certain lady, and his hat was on the table beside him, and it wanted brushing badly, and he was in tears. Me? I saw him with that lady in various attitudes and emotions – I never felt so detached before... I saw him hurrying off to Lympne to write a play, and accosting Cavor, and in his shirt sleeves working at the sphere, and walking out to Canterbury because he was afraid to come! Me? I did not believe it.

I still reasoned that all this was hallucination due to my solitude, and the fact that I had lost all weight and sense of resistance. I endeavoured to recover that sense by banging myself about the sphere, by pinching my hands and clasping them together. Among other things, I lit the light, captured that torn copy of *Lloyd's*, and read those convincingly realistic advertisements about the Cutaway bicycle, and the gentleman of private means, and the lady in distress who was selling those "forks and spoons." There was no doubt they existed surely enough, and, said I, "This is your world, and you are Bedford, and you are going back to live among things like that for all the rest of your life." But the doubts within me could still argue: "It is not you that is reading, it is Bedford, but you are not Bedford, you know. That's just where the mistake comes in."

"Confound it!" I cried; "and if I am not Bedford, what am I?"

But in that direction no light was forthcoming, though the strangest fancies came drifting into my brain, queer remote suspicions, like shadows seen from far away... Do you know, I had a sort of idea that really I was something quite outside not only the world, but all worlds, and out of space and time, and that this poor Bedford was just a peephole through which I looked at life?...

Bedford! However I disavowed him, there I was most certainly bound up with him, and I knew that wherever or whatever I might be, I must needs feel the stress of his desires, and sympathise with all his joys and sorrows until his life should end. And with the dying of Bedford – what then?...

Enough of this remarkable phase of my experiences! I tell it here simply to show how one's isolation and departure from this planet touched not only the functions and feeling of every organ of the body, but indeed also the very fabric of the mind, with strange and unanticipated disturbances. All through the major portion of that vast space journey I hung thinking of such immaterial things as these, hung dissociated and apathetic, a cloudy megalomaniac, as it were, amidst the stars and planets in the void of space; and not only the world to which I was returning, but the blue-lit caverns of the Selenites, their helmet faces, their gigantic and wonderful machines, and the fate of Cavor, dragged helpless into that world, seemed infinitely minute and altogether trivial things to me.

Until at last I began to feel the pull of the earth upon my being, drawing me back again to the life that is real for men. And then, indeed, it grew clearer and clearer to me that I was quite certainly Bedford after all, and returning after amazing adventures to this world of ours, and with a life that I was very likely to lose in this return. I set myself to puzzle out the conditions under which I must fall to earth.

# CHAPTER TWENTY-ONE

## Mr Bedford at Littlestone

My line of flight was about parallel with the surface as I came into the upper air. The temperature of the sphere began to rise forthwith. I knew it behoved me to drop at once. Far below me, in a darkling twilight, stretched a great expanse of sea. I opened every window I could, and fell – out of sunshine into evening, and out of evening into night. Vaster grew the earth and vaster, swallowing up the stars, and the silvery translucent starlit veil of cloud it wore spread out to catch me. At last the world seemed no longer a sphere but flat, and then concave. It was no longer a planet in the sky, but the world of Man. I shut all but an inch or so of earthward window, and dropped with a slackening velocity. The broadening water, now so near that I could see the dark glitter of the waves, rushed up to meet me. The sphere became very hot. I snapped the last strip of window, and sat scowling and biting my knuckles, waiting for the impact...

The sphere hit the water with a huge splash: it must have sent it fathoms high. At the splash I flung the Cavorite shutters open. Down I went, but slower and slower, and then I felt the sphere pressing against my feet, and so drove up again as a bubble drives. And at the last I was floating and rocking upon the surface of the sea, and my journey in space was at an end.

The night was ·dark and overcast. Two yellow pinpoints far away showed the passing of a ship, and nearer was a red glare that came and went. Had not the electricity of my glow-lamp exhausted itself, I could have got picked up that night. In spite of the inordinate fatigue I was beginning to feel, I was excited now, and for a time hopeful, in a feverish, impatient way, that so my travelling might end.

But at last I ceased to move about, and sat, wrists on knees, staring at a distant red light. It swayed up and down, rocking, rocking. My excitement passed. I realised I had yet to spend another night at least in the sphere. I perceived myself infinitely heavy and fatigued. And so I fell asleep.

A change in my rhythmic motion awakened me. I peered through the refracting glass, and saw that I had come aground upon a huge shallow of sand. Far away I seemed to see houses and trees, and seaward a curve, vague distortion of a ship hung between sea and sky.

I stood up and staggered. My one desire was to emerge. The manhole was upward, and I wrestled with the screw. Slowly I opened the manhole. At last the air was singing in again as once it had sung out. But this time I did not wait until the pressure was adjusted. In another moment I had the weight of the window on my hands, and I was open, wide open, to the old familiar sky of earth.

The air hit me on the chest so that I gasped. I dropped the glass screw. I cried out, put my hands to my chest, and sat down. For a time I was in pain. Then I took deep breaths. At last I could rise and move about again.

I tried to thrust my head through the manhole, and the sphere rolled over. It was as though something had lugged my head down directly it emerged. I ducked back sharply, or I should have been pinned face under water. After some wriggling and shoving I managed to crawl out upon sand, over which the retreating waves still came and went.

I did not attempt to stand up. It seemed to me that my body must be suddenly changed to lead. Mother Earth had her grip on me now – no Cavorite intervening. I sat down heedless of the water that came over my feet.

It was dawn, a gray dawn, rather overcast but showing here and there a long patch of greenish gray. Some way out a ship was lying at anchor, a pale silhouette of a ship with one yellow light. The water came rippling in in long shallow waves. Away to the right curved the land, a shingle bank with little hovels, and at last a lighthouse, a sailing mark and a point. Inland stretched a space of level sand, broken here and there by pools of water, and ending a mile away perhaps in a low shore of scrub. To the north-east some isolated watering-place was visible, a row of gaunt lodging-houses, the tallest things that I could see on earth, dull dabs against the brightening sky. What strange men can have reared these vertical piles in such an amplitude of space I do not know. There they are, like pieces of Brighton lost in the waste.

For a long time I sat there, yawning and rubbing my face. At last I struggled to rise. It made me feel that I was lifting a weight. I stood up.

I stared at the distant houses. For the first time since our starvation in the crater I thought of earthly food. "Bacon," I whispered, "eggs. Good toast and good coffee... And how the devil am I going to get all this stuff to Lympne?" I wondered

189

where I was. It was an east shore anyhow, and I had seen Europe before I dropped.

I heard footsteps scrunching in the sand, and a little round-faced, friendly-looking man in flannels, with a bathing towel wrapped about his shoulders, and his bathing dress over his arm, appeared up the beach. I knew instantly that I must be in England. He was staring most intently at the sphere and me. He advanced staring. I dare say I looked a ferocious savage enough – dirty, unkempt, to an indescribable degree; but it did not occur to me at the time. He stopped at a distance of twenty yards. "Hul-lo, my man!" he said doubtfully.

"Hullo yourself!" said I.

He advanced, reassured by that. "What on earth is that thing?" he asked.

"Can you tell me where I am?" I asked.

"That's Littlestone," he said, pointing to the houses; "and that's Dungeness! Have you just landed? What's that thing you've got? Some sort of machine?"

"Yes."

"Have you floated ashore? Have you been wrecked or something? What is it?"

I meditated swiftly. I made an estimate of the little man's appearance as he drew nearer. "By Jove!" he said, "you've had a time of it! I thought you – Well – Where were you cast away? Is that thing a sort of floating thing for saving life?"

I decided to take that line for the present. I made a few vague affirmatives. "I want help," I said hoarsely. "I want to get some stuff up the beach – stuff I can't very well leave about." I became aware of three other pleasant-looking young men with towels, blazers, and straw hats, coming down the sands towards me. Evidently the early bathing section of this Littlestone.

"Help!" said the young man: "rather!" He became vaguely active. "What particularly do you want done?" He turned round and gesticulated. The three young men accelerated their pace. In a minute they were about me, plying me with questions I was indisposed to answer. "I'll tell all that later," I said. "I'm dead beat. I'm a rag."

"Come up to the hotel," said the foremost little man. "We'll look after that thing there."

I hesitated. "I can't," I said. "In that sphere there's two big bars of gold."

They looked incredulously at one another, then at me with a new inquiry. I went to the sphere, stooped, crept in, and presently they had the Selenites' crowbars and the broken chain before them. If I had not been so horribly fagged I could have laughed at them. It was like kittens round a beetle. They didn't know what to do with the stuff. The fat little man stooped and lifted the end of one of the bars, and then dropped it with a grunt. Then they all did.

"It's lead, or gold!" said one.

"Oh, it's *gold!*" said another.

"Gold, right enough," said the third.

Then they all stared at me, and then they all stared at the ship lying at anchor.

"I say!" cried the little man. "But where did you get that?"

I was too tired to keep up a lie. "I got it in the moon."

I saw them stare at one another.

"Look here!" said I, "I'm not going to argue now. Help me carry these lumps of gold up to the hotel – I guess, with rests, two of you can manage one, and I'll trail this chain thing – and I'll tell you more when I've had some food."

"And how about that thing?"

"It won't hurt there," I said. "Anyhow – confound it! – it must stop there now. If the tide comes up, it will float all right."

And in a state of enormous wonderment, these young men most obediently hoisted my treasures on their shoulders, and with limbs that felt like lead I headed a sort of procession towards that distant fragment of "sea-front." Half-way there we were reinforced by two awe-stricken little girls with spades, and later a lean little boy, with a penetrating sniff, appeared. He was, I remember, wheeling a bicycle, and he accompanied us at a distance of about a hundred yards on our right flank, and then I suppose, gave us up as uninteresting, mounted his bicycle and rode off over the level sands in the direction of the sphere.

I glanced back after him.

"*He* won't touch it," said the stout young man reassuringly, and I was only too willing to be reassured.

At first something of the gray of the morning was in my mind, but presently the sun disengaged itself from the level clouds of the horizon and lit the world, and turned the leaden sea to glittering waters. My spirits rose. A sense of the vast importance of the things I had done and had yet to do came with the sunlight into my mind. I laughed aloud as the foremost man staggered under my gold. When indeed I took my place in the world, how amazed the world would be!

If it had not been for my inordinate fatigue, the landlord of the Littlestone hotel would have been amusing, as he hesitated between my gold and my respectable company on the one hand and my filthy appearance on the other. But at last I found myself in a terrestrial bathroom once more with warm water to wash myself with, and a change of raiment, preposterously small indeed, but anyhow clean, that the genial little man had lent me. He lent me a razor too, but I could not screw up my resolution to attack even the outposts of the bristling beard that covered my face.

I sat down to an English breakfast and ate with a sort of languid appetite – an appetite many weeks old and very decrepit – and stirred myself to answer the questions of the four young men. And I told them the truth.

"Well," said I, "as you press me – I got it in the moon."

"The moon?"

"Yes, the moon in the sky."

"But how do you mean?"

"What I say, confound it!"

"Then you have just come from the moon?"

"Exactly! through space – in that ball." And I took a delicious mouthful of egg. I made a private note that when I went back to the moon I would take a box of eggs.

I could see clearly that they did not believe one word what I told them, but evidently they considered me the most respectable liar they had ever met. They glanced at one another, and then concentrated the fire of their eyes on me. I fancy they expected a clue to me in the way I helped myself to salt. They seemed to find something significant in my peppering my egg. These strangely shaped masses of gold they had staggered under held their minds. There the lumps lay in front of me, each worth thousands of pounds, and as impossible for anyone to steal as a house or a piece of land. As I looked at their curious faces over my coffee-cup, I realised something of the enormous wilderness of explanations into which I should have to wander to render myself comprehensible again.

"You don't *really* mean – " began the youngest young man, in the tone of one who speaks to an obstinate child.

"Just pass me that toast-rack," I said, and shut him up completely.

"But look here, I say," began one of the others. "We're not going to believe that, you know."

"Ah, well," said I, and shrugged my shoulders.

"He doesn't want to tell us," said the youngest young man in a stage aside; and then, with an appearance of great *sang-froid*, "You don't mind if I take a cigarette?"

I waved him a cordial assent, and proceeded with my breakfast. Two of the others went and looked out of the farther window and talked inaudibly. I was struck by a thought. "The tide," I said, "is running out?"

There was a pause, a doubt who should answer me. "It's near the ebb," said the fat little man.

"Well, anyhow," I said, "it won't float far."

I decapitated my third egg, and began a little speech. "Look here," I said. "Please don't imagine I'm surly or telling you uncivil lies, or anything of that sort. I'm forced almost, to be a little short and mysterious. I can quite understand this is as queer as it can be, and that your imaginations must be going it. I can assure you, you're in at a memorable time. But I can't make it clear to you now – it's impossible. I give you my word of honour I've come from the moon, and that's all I can tell you... All the same, I'm tremendously obliged to you, you know, tremendously. I hope that my manner hasn't in any way given you offence."

"Oh, not in the least!" said the youngest young man affably. "We can quite understand," and staring hard at me all the time, he heeled his chair back until it very nearly upset, and recovered with some exertion. "Not a bit of it," said the fat young man. "Don't you imagine *that!*" and they all got up and dispersed, and walked about and lit cigarettes, and generally tried to show they were perfectly amiable and disengaged, and entirely free from the slightest curiosity about me and the sphere. "I'm going to keep an eye on that ship out there all the same," I heard one of them remarking in an undertone. If only they could have forced themselves to it, they would, I believe, even have gone out and left me. I went on with my third egg.

"The weather," the fat little man remarked presently, "has been immense, has it not? I don't know *when* we have had such a summer..."

Phoo – whizz! Like a tremendous rocket!

And somewhere a window was broken...

"What's that?" said I.

"It isn't – ?" cried the little man, and rushed to the corner window.

All the others rushed to the window likewise. I sat staring at them.

Suddenly I leapt up, knocked over my third egg, rushed for the window also. I had just thought of something. "Nothing to be seen there," cried the little man, rushing for the door.

"It's that boy!" I cried, bawling in hoarse fury; "it's that accursed boy!" and turning about I pushed the waiter aside – he was just bringing me some more toast – and rushed violently out of the room and down and out upon the queer little esplanade in front of the hotel.

The sea, which had been smooth, was rough now with hurrying cat's-paws, and all about where the sphere had been was tumbled water like the wake of a ship. Above, a little puff of cloud whirled like dispersing smoke, and the three or four people on the beach were staring up with interrogative faces towards the point of that unexpected report. And that was all! Boots and waiter and the four young men in blazers came rushing out behind me. Shouts came from windows and doors, and all sorts of worrying people came into sight – agape.

For a time I stood there, too overwhelmed by this new development to think of the people.

At first I was too stunned to see the thing as any definite disaster – I was just stunned, as a man is by some accidental violent blow. It is only afterwards he begins to appreciate his specific injury.

"Good Lord!"

I felt as though somebody was pouring funk out of a can down the back of my neck. My legs became feeble. I had got the first intimation of what the disaster meant for me. There was that confounded boy – sky high! I was utterly "left." There was the gold in the coffee-room – my only possession on earth. How would it all work out? The general effect was of a gigantic unmanageable confusion.

"I say," said the voice of the little man behind. "I *say*, you know."

I wheeled about, and there were twenty or thirty people, a sort of irregular investment of people, all bombarding me with dumb interrogation, with infinite doubt and suspicion. I felt the compulsion of their eyes intolerably. I groaned aloud.

"I *can't!*" I shouted. "I tell you I can't! I'm not equal to it! You must puzzle and – and be damned to you!"

I gesticulated convulsively. He receded a step as though I had threatened him. I made a bolt through them into the hotel. I charged back into the coffee-room, rang the bell furiously. I gripped the waiter as he entered. "D'ye hear?" I shouted. "Get help and carry these bars up to my room right away."

He failed to understand me, and I shouted and raved at him. A scared-looking little old man in a green apron appeared, and further two of the young men in flannels. I made a dash at them and commandeered their services. As soon as the gold was in my room I felt free to quarrel. "Now get out," I shouted; "all of you get out if you don't want to see a man go mad before your eyes!" And I helped the waiter by the shoulder as he hesitated in the doorway. And then, as soon as I had the door locked on them all, I tore off the little man's clothes again, shied them right and left, and got into bed forthwith. And there I lay swearing and panting and cooling for a very long time.

At last I was calm enough to get out of bed and ring up the round-eyed waiter for a flannel nightshirt, a soda and whisky, and some good cigars. And these things being procured me, after an exasperating delay that drove me several times to the bell, I locked the door again and proceeded very deliberately to look the entire situation in the face.

The net result of the great experiment presented itself as an absolute failure. It was a rout, and I was the sole survivor. It was an absolute collapse, and this was the final disaster. There was nothing for it but to save myself, and as much as I could in the way of prospects from our *débâcle*. At one fatal crowning blow all my vague resolutions of return and recovery had vanished. My

197

intention of going back to the moon, of getting a sphereful of gold, and afterwards of having a fragment of Cavorite analysed and so recovering the great secret – perhaps, finally, even of recovering Cavor's body – all these ideas vanished altogether.

I was the sole survivor, and that was all.

I think that going to bed was one of the luckiest ideas I have ever had in an emergency. I really believe I should either have got loose-headed or done some fatal, indiscreet thing. But there, locked in and secure from all interruptions, I could think out the position in all its bearings and make my arrangements at leisure.

Of course, it was quite clear to me what had happened to the boy. He had crawled into the sphere, meddled with the studs, shut the Cavorite windows, and gone up. It was highly improbable he had screwed the manhole stopper, and, even if he had, the chances were a thousand to one against his getting back. It was fairly evident that he would gravitate with my bales to somewhere near the middle of the sphere and remain there, and so cease to be a legitimate terrestrial interest, however remarkable he might seem to the inhabitants of some remote quarter of space. I very speedily convinced myself on that point. And as for any responsibility I might have in the matter, the more I reflected upon that, the clearer it became that if only I kept quiet about things, I need not trouble myself about that. If I was faced by sorrowing parents demanding their lost boy, I had merely to demand my lost sphere – or ask them what they meant. At first I had had a vision of weeping parents and guardians, and all sorts of complications; but now I saw that I simply had to keep my mouth shut, and nothing in that way could arise. And, indeed, the more I lay and smoked and thought, the more evident became the wisdom of impenetrability.

It is within the right of every British citizen, provided he does not commit damage nor indecorum, to appear suddenly wherever he pleases, and as ragged and filthy as he pleases, and with whatever amount of virgin gold he sees fit to encumber himself, and no one has any right at all to hinder and detain him in this procedure. I formulated that at last to myself, and repeated it over as a sort of private Magna Charta of my liberty.

Once I had put that issue on one side, I could take up and consider in an equable manner certain considerations I had scarcely dared to think of before, namely, those arising out of the circumstances of my bankruptcy. But now, looking at this matter calmly and at leisure, I could see that if only I suppressed my identity by a temporary assumption of some less well-known name, and if I retained the two months' beard that had grown upon me, the risks of any annoyance from the spiteful creditor to whom I have already alluded became very small indeed. From that to a definite course of rational worldly action was plain sailing. It was all amazingly petty, no doubt, but what was there remaining for me to do?

Whatever I did I was resolved that I would keep myself level and right side up.

I ordered up writing materials, and addressed a letter to the New Romney Bank – the nearest, the waiter informed me – telling the manager I wished to open an account with him, and requesting him to send two trustworthy persons properly authenticated in a cab with a good horse to fetch some hundred-weight of gold with which I happened to be encumbered. I signed the letter "Blake," which seemed to me to be a thoroughly respectable sort of name. This done, I got a Folkstone Blue Book, picked out an outfitter, and asked him to send a cutter to measure me for a dark tweed suit, ordering at the same time a valise, dressing bag, brown boots, shirts, hat (to fit), and so forth; and from a watchmaker I also ordered a watch. And these letters being despatched, I had up as good a lunch as the hotel could give, and then lay smoking a cigar, as calm and ordinary as possible, until in accordance with my instructions two duly authenticated clerks came from the bank and weighed and took away my gold. After which I pulled the clothes over my ears in order to drown any knocking, and went very comfortably to sleep.

I went to sleep. No doubt it was a prosaic thing for the first man back from the moon to do, and I can imagine that the young and imaginative reader will find my behaviour disappointing. But I was horribly fatigued and bothered, and, confound it! what else was there to do? There certainly was not the remotest chance of my being believed, if I had told my story then, and it would certainly have subjected me to intolerable annoyances. I went to sleep. When at last I woke up again I was ready to face the world, as I have always been accustomed to face it since I came to years of discretion. And so I got away to Italy, and there it is I am writing this story. If the world will not have it as fact, then the world may take it as fiction. It is no concern of mine.

And now that the account is finished, I am amazed to think how completely this adventure is gone and done with. Everybody believes that Cavor was a not very brilliant scientific experimenter who blew up his house and himself at Lympne, and they explain the bang that followed my arrival at Littlestone by a reference to the experiments with explosives that are going on continually at the government establishment of Lydd, two miles away. I must confess that hitherto I have not acknowledged my share in the disappearance of Master Tommy Simmons, which was that little boy's name. That, perhaps, may prove a difficult item of corroboration to explain away. They account for my appearance in rags with two bars of indisputable gold upon the Littlestone beach in various ingenious ways – it doesn't worry me what they think of me. They say I have strung all these things together to avoid being questioned too closely as to the source of my wealth. I would like to see the man who could invent a story that would hold together like this one. Well, they must take it as fiction – there it is.

I have told my story – and now, I suppose, I have to take up the worries of this terrestrial life again. Even if one has been to the moon, one has still to earn a living. So I am working here at Amalfi, on the scenario of that play I sketched before Cavor came walking into my world, and I am trying to piece my life together as it was before ever I saw him. I must confess that I find it hard to keep my mind on the play when the moonshine comes into my room. It is full moon here, and last night I was out on the pergola for hours, staring away at the shining blankness that hides so much. Imagine it! tables and chairs, and trestles and bars of gold! Confound it! – if only one could hit on that Cavorite again! But a thing like that doesn't come twice in a life. Here I am, a little better off than I was at Lympne, and that is all. And Cavor has committed suicide in a more elaborate way than any human being ever did before. So the story closes as finally and completely as a dream. It fits in so little with all the other things of life, so much of it is so utterly remote from all human experience, the leaping, the eating, the breathing, and these weightless times, that indeed there are moments when, in spite of my moon gold, I do more than half believe myself that the whole thing was a dream...

# CHAPTER TWENTY-TWO

## The Astonishing Communication of
## Mr Julius Wendigee

When I had finished my account of my return to the earth at Littlestone, I wrote, "The End", made a flourish, and threw my pen aside, fully believing that the whole story of the First Men in the Moon was done. Not only had I done this, but I had placed my manuscript in the hands of a literary agent, had permitted it to be sold, had seen the greater portion of it appear in the *Strand Magazine*, and was setting to work again upon the scenario of the play I had commenced at Lympne before I realised that the end was not yet. And then, following me from Amalfi to Algiers, there reached me (it is now about six months ago) one of the most astounding communications I have ever been fated to receive. Briefly, it informed me that Mr Julius Wendigee, a Dutch electrician, who has been experimenting with certain apparatus akin to the apparatus used by Mr Tesla in America, in the hope of discovering some method of communication with Mars, was receiving day by day a curiously fragmentary message in English, which was indisputably emanating from Mr Cavor in the moon.

At first I thought the thing was an elaborate practical joke by someone who had seen the manuscript of my narrative. I answered Mr Wendigee jestingly, but he replied in a manner that put such suspicion altogether aside, and in a state of inconceivable excitement I hurried from Algiers to the little observatory upon the St Gothard in which he was working. In the presence of his record and his appliances – and above all of the messages from Cavor that were coming to hand – my lingering doubts vanished. I decided at once to accept a proposal he made to me to remain with him, assisting him to take down the record from day to day, and endeavouring with him to send a message back to the moon. Cavor, we learnt, was not only alive, but free, in the midst of an almost inconceivable community of these ant-like beings, these ant-men, in the blue darkness of the lunar caves. He was lamed, it seemed, but otherwise in quite good health – in better health, he distinctly said, than he usually enjoyed on earth. He had had a fever, but it had left no bad effects. But curiously enough he seemed to be labouring under a conviction that I was either dead in the moon crater or lost in the deep of space.

His message began to be received by Mr Wendigee when that gentleman was engaged in quite a different investigation. The reader will no doubt recall the little excitement that began the century, arising out of an announcement by Mr Nikola Tesla, the American electrical celebrity, that he had received a message from Mars. His announcement renewed attention to a fact that had long been familiar to scientific people, namely: that from some unknown source in space, waves of electro-magnetic disturbance, entirely similar to those used by Signor Marconi for his wireless telegraphy, are constantly reaching the earth. Besides Tesla quite a number of other observers have been engaged in perfecting apparatus for receiving and recording these vibrations, though few would go so far as to consider them actual messages from some extra-terrestrial sender. Among that few, however, we must certainly count Mr Wendigee. Ever since 1898 he had devoted himself almost entirely to this subject, and being a man of ample means he had erected an observatory on the flanks of Monte Rosa, in a position singularly adapted in every way for such observations.

My scientific attainments, I must admit, are not great, but so far as they enable me to judge, Mr Wendigee's contrivances for detecting and recording any disturbances in the electro-magnetic conditions of space are singularly original and ingenious. And by a happy combination of circumstances they were set up and in operation about two months before Cavor made his first attempt to call up the earth. Consequently we have fragments of his communication even from the beginning. Unhappily, they are only fragments, and the most momentous of all the things that he had to tell humanity – the instructions, that is, for the making of Cavorite, if, indeed, he ever transmitted them – have throbbed themselves away unrecorded into space. We never succeeded in getting a response back to Cavor. He was unable to tell, therefore, what we had received or what we had missed; nor, indeed, did he certainly know that anyone on earth was really aware of his efforts to reach us. And the persistence he displayed in sending eighteen long descriptions of lunar affairs – as they would be if we had them complete – shows how much his mind must have turned back towards his native planet since he left it two years ago.

You can imagine how amazed Mr Wendigee must have been when he discovered his record of electro-magnetic disturbances interlaced by Cavor's straightforward English. Mr Wendigee knew nothing of our wild journey moonward, and suddenly – this English out of the void!

It is well the reader should understand the conditions under which it would seem these messages were sent. Somewhere within the moon Cavor certainly had access for a time to a considerable amount of electrical apparatus, and it would seem he rigged up – perhaps furtively – a transmitting arrangement of the Marconi type. This he was able to operate at irregular intervals: sometimes for only half an hour or so, sometimes for three or four hours at a stretch. At these times he transmitted his earthward message, regardless of the fact that the relative position of the moon and points upon the earth's surface is constantly altering. As a consequence of this and of the necessary imperfections of our recording instruments his communication comes and goes in our records in an extremely fitful manner; it becomes blurred; it "fades out" in a mysterious and altogether exasperating way. And added to this is the fact that he was not an expert operator; he had partly forgotten, or never completely mastered, the code in general use, and as he became fatigued he dropped words and misspelt in a curious manner.

Altogether we have probably lost quite half of the communications he made, and much we have is damaged, broken, and partly effaced. In the abstract that follows the reader must be prepared therefore for a considerable amount of break, hiatus, and change of topic. Mr Wendigee and I are collaborating in a complete and annotated edition of the Cavor record, which we hope to publish, together with a detailed account of the instruments employed, beginning with the first volume in January next. That will be the full and scientific report, of which this is only the popular first transcript. But here we give at least sufficient to complete the story I have told, and to give the broad outlines of the state of that other world so near, so akin, and yet so dissimilar to our own.

# CHAPTER TWENTY-THREE

## An Abstract of the Six Messages First Received
## from Mr Cavor

The two earlier messages of Mr Cavor may very well be reserved for that larger volume. They simply tell, with greater brevity and with a difference in several details that is interesting, but not of any vital importance, the bare facts of the making of the sphere and our departure from the world. Throughout, Cavor speaks of me as a man who is dead, but with a curious change of temper as he approaches our landing on the moon. "Poor Bedford," he says of me, and "this poor young man"; and he blames himself for inducing a young man, "by no means well equipped for such adventures," to leave a planet "on which he was indisputably fitted to succeed" on so precarious a mission. I think he underrates the part my energy and practical capacity played in bringing about the realisation of his theoretical sphere. "We arrived," he says, with no more account of our passage through space than if we had made a journey of common occurrence in a railway train.

And then he becomes increasingly unfair to me. Unfair, indeed, to an extent I should not have expected in a man trained in the search for truth. Looking back over my previously written account of these things, I must insist that I have been altogether juster to Cavor than he has been to me. I have extenuated little and suppressed nothing. But his account is:-

"It speedily became apparent that the entire strangeness of our circumstances and surroundings – great loss of weight, attenuated but highly oxygenated air, consequent exaggeration of the results of muscular effort, rapid development of weird plants from obscure spores, lurid sky – was exciting my companion unduly. On the moon his character seemed to deteriorate. He became impulsive, rash, and quarrelsome. In a little while his folly in devouring some gigantic vesicles and his consequent intoxication led to our capture by the Selenites – before we had had the slightest opportunity of properly observing their ways…"

(He says, you observe, nothing of his own concession to these same "vesicles.")

And he goes on from that point to say that "We came to a difficult passage with them, and Bedford mistaking certain gestures of theirs" – pretty gestures they were! – "gave way to a panic violence. He ran amuck, killed three, and perforce I had to flee with him after the outrage. Subsequently we fought with a number who endeavoured to bar our way, and slew seven or eight more. It says much for the tolerance of these beings that on my recapture I was not instantly slain. We made our way to the exterior and separated in the crater of our arrival, to increase our chances of recovering our sphere. But presently I came upon a body of Selenites, led by two who were curiously different, even in form, from any of these we had seen hitherto, with larger heads and smaller bodies, and much more elaborately wrapped about. And after evading them for some time I fell into a

210

crevasse, cut my head rather badly, and displaced my patella, and, finding crawling very painful, decided to surrender – if they would still permit me to do so. This they did, and, perceiving my helpless condition, carried me with them again into the moon. And of Bedford I have heard or seen nothing more, nor, so far as I can gather, has any Selenite. Either the night overtook him in the crater, or else, which is more probable, he found the sphere, and, desiring to steal a march upon me, made off with it – only, I fear, to find it uncontrollable, and to meet a more lingering fate in outer space."

And with that Cavor dismisses me and goes onto more interesting topics. I dislike the idea of seeming to use my position as his editor to deflect his story in my own interest, but I am obliged to protest here against the turn he gives these occurrences. He says nothing about that gasping message on the blood-stained paper in which he told, or attempted to tell, a very different story. The dignified self-surrender is an altogether new view of the affair that has come to him, I must insist, since he began to feel secure among the lunar people; and as for the "stealing a march" conception, I am quite willing to let the reader decide between us on what he has before him. I know I am not a model man – I have made no pretence to be. But am I *that*?

However, that is the sum of my wrongs. From this point I can edit Cavor with an untroubled mind, for he mentions me no more.

It would seem the Selenites who had come upon him carried him to some point in the interior down "a great shaft" by means of what he describes as "a sort of balloon." We gather from the rather confused passage in which he describes this, and from a number of chance allusions and hints in other and subsequent messages, that this "great shaft" is one of an enormous system of artificial shafts that run, each from what is called a lunar "crater," downwards for very nearly a hundred miles towards the central portion of our satellite. These shafts communicate by transverse tunnels, they throw out abysmal caverns and expand into great globular places; the whole of the moon's substance for a hundred miles inward, indeed, is a mere sponge of rock. "Partly," says Cavor, "this sponginess is natural, but very largely it is due to the enormous industry of the Selenites in the past. The enormous circular mounds of the excavated rock and earth it is that form these great circles about the tunnels known to earthly astronomers (misled by a false analogy) as volcanoes."

It was down this shaft they took him, in this "sort of balloon" he speaks of, at first into an inky blackness and then into a region of continually increasing phosphorescence. Cavor's despatches show him to be curiously regardless of detail for a scientific man, but we gather that this light was due to the streams and cascades of water – "no doubt containing some phosphorescent organism" – that flowed ever more abundantly downward towards the Central Sea. And as he descended, he says, "The Selenites also became luminous." And at last far below him he saw, as it were, a lake of heatless fire, the waters of the Central Sea, glowing and eddying in strange perturbation, "like luminous blue milk that is just on the boil."

"This Lunar Sea," says Cavor, in a later passage "is not a stagnant ocean; a solar tide sends it in a perpetual flow around the lunar axis, and strange storms and boilings and rushings of its waters occur, and at times cold winds and thunderings that ascend out of it into the busy ways of the great ant-hill above. It is only when the water is in motion that it gives out light; in its rare seasons of calm it is black. Commonly, when one sees it, its waters rise and fall in an oily swell, and flakes and big rafts of shining, bubbly foam drift with the sluggish, faintly glowing current. The Selenites navigate its cavernous straits and lagoons in little shallow boats of a canoe-like shape; and even before my journey to the galleries about the Grand Lunar, who is Master of the Moon, I was permitted to make a brief excursion on its waters.

"The caverns and passages are naturally very tortuous. A large proportion of these ways are known only to expert pilots among the fishermen, and not infrequently Selenites are lost for ever in their labyrinths. In their remoter recesses, I am told, strange creatures lurk, some of them terrible and dangerous creatures that all the science of the moon has been unable to exterminate. There is particularly the Rapha, an inextricable mass of clutching tentacles that one hacks to pieces only to multiply; and the Tzee, a darting creature that is never seen, so subtly and suddenly does it slay…"

He gives us a gleam of description.

"I was reminded on this excursion of what I have read of the Mammoth Caves; if only I had had a yellow flambeau instead of the pervading blue light, and a solid-looking boatman with an oar instead of a scuttle-faced Selenite working an engine at the back of the canoe, I could have imagined I had suddenly got back to earth. The rocks about us were very various, sometimes black, sometimes pale blue and veined, and once they flashed and glittered as though we had come into a mine of sapphires. And below one saw the ghostly phosphorescent fishes flash and vanish in the hardly less phosphorescent deep. Then, presently, a long

213

ultra-marine vista down the turgid stream of one of the channels of traffic, and a landing stage, and then, perhaps, a glimpse up the enormous crowded shaft of one of the vertical ways.

"In one great place heavy with glistening stalactites a number of boats were fishing. We went alongside one of these and watched the long-armed Selenites winding in a net. They were little, hunchbacked insects, with very strong arms, short, bandy legs, and crinkled face-masks. As they pulled at it that net seemed the heaviest thing I had come upon in the moon; it was loaded with weights – no doubt of gold – and it took a long time to draw, for in those waters the larger and more edible fish lurk deep. The fish in the net came up like a blue moonrise – a blaze of darting, tossing blue.

"Among their catch was a many-tentaculate, evil-eyed black thing, ferociously active, whose appearance they greeted with shrieks and twitters, and which with quick, nervous movements they hacked to pieces by means of little hatchets. All its dissevered limbs continued to lash and writhe in a vicious manner. Afterwards, when fever had hold of me, I dreamt again and again of that bitter, furious creature rising so vigorous and active out of the unknown sea. It was the most active and malignant thing of all the living creatures I have yet seen in this world inside the moon...

"The surface of this sea must be very nearly two hundred miles (if not more) below the level of the moon's exterior; all the cities of the moon lie, I learnt, immediately above this Central Sea, in such cavernous spaces and artificial galleries as I have described, and they communicate with the exterior by enormous vertical shafts which open invariably in what are called by earthly astronomers the 'craters' of the moon. The lid covering one such aperture I had already seen during the wanderings that had preceded my capture.

"Upon the condition of the less central portion of the moon I have not yet arrived at very precise knowledge. There is an enormous system of caverns in which the mooncalves shelter during the night; and there are abattoirs and the like – in one of these it was that I and Bedford fought with the Selenite butchers – and I have since seen balloons laden with meat descending out of the upper dark. I have as yet scarcely learnt as much of these things as a Zulu in London would learn about the British corn supplies in the same time. It is clear, however, that these vertical shafts and the vegetation of the surface must play an essential role in ventilating and keeping fresh the atmosphere of the moon. At one time, and particularly on my first emergence from my prison, there was certainly a cold wind blowing *down* the shaft, and later there was a kind of sirocco upward that corresponded with my fever. For at the end of about three weeks I fell ill of an indefinable sort of fever, and in spite of sleep and the quinine tabloids that very fortunately I had brought in my pocket, I remained ill and fretting miserably, almost to the time when I was taken into the presence of the Grand Lunar, who is Master of the Moon.

"I will not dilate on the wretchedness of my condition," he remarks, "during those days of ill-health." And he goes on with great amplitude with details I omit here. "My temperature," he concludes, "kept abnormally high for a long time, and I lost all desire for food. I had stagnant waking intervals, and sleep tormented by dreams, and at one phase I was, I remember, so weak as to be earth-sick and almost hysterical. I longed almost intolerably for colour to break the everlasting blue..."

He reverts again presently to the topic of this sponge caught lunar atmosphere. I am told by astronomers and physicists that all he tells is in absolute accordance with what was already known of the moon's condition. Had earthly astronomers had the courage and imagination to push home a bold induction, says Mr Wendigee, they might have foretold almost everything that Cavor has to say of the general structure of the moon. They know now pretty certainly that moon and earth are not so much satellite and primary as smaller and greater sisters, made out of one mass, and consequently made of the same material. And since the density of the moon is only three-fifths that of the earth, there can be nothing for it but that she is hollowed out by a great system of caverns. There was no necessity, said Sir Jabez Flap, FRS, that most entertaining exponent of the facetious side of the stars, that we should ever have gone to the moon to find out such easy inferences, and points the pun with an allusion to Gruyère, but he certainly might have announced his knowledge of the hollowness of the moon before. And if the moon is hollow, then the apparent absence of air and water is, of course, quite easily explained. The sea lies within at the bottom of the caverns, and the air travels through the great sponge of galleries, in accordance with simple physical laws. The caverns of the moon, on the whole, are very windy places. As the sunlight comes round the moon the air in the outer galleries on that side is heated, its pressure increases, some flows out on the exterior and mingles with the evaporating air of the craters (where the plants remove its carbonic acid), while the greater portion flows round through the galleries to replace the shrinking air of the cooling side that the sunlight has left. There is, therefore, a constant eastward breeze in the air of the outer galleries, and an upflow during the lunar day up the shafts, complicated, of course, very greatly by the varying shape of the galleries, and the ingenious contrivances of the Selenite mind...

# CHAPTER TWENTY-FOUR

## The Natural History of the Selenites

The messages of Cavor from the sixth up to the sixteenth are for the most part so much broken, and they abound so in repetitions, that they scarcely form a consecutive narrative. They will be given in full, of course, in the scientific report, but here it will be far more convenient to continue simply to abstract and quote as in the former chapter. We have subjected every word to a keen critical scrutiny, and my own brief memories and impressions of lunar things have been of inestimable help in interpreting what would otherwise have been impenetrably dark. And, naturally, as living beings, our interest centres far more upon the strange community of lunar insects in which he was living, it would seem, as an honoured guest than upon the mere physical condition of their world.

I have already made it clear, I think, that the Selenites I saw resembled man in maintaining the erect attitude, and in having four limbs, and I have compared the general appearance of their heads and the jointing of their limbs to that of insects. I have mentioned, too, the peculiar consequence of the smaller gravitation of the moon on their fragile slightness. Cavor confirms me upon all these points. He calls them "animals," though of course they fall under no division of the classification of earthly creatures, and he points out "the insect type of anatomy had, fortunately for men, never exceeded a relatively very small size on earth." The largest terrestrial insects, living or extinct, do not, as a matter of fact, measure 6in. in length; "but here, against the lesser gravitation of the moon, a creature certainly as much an insect as vertebrate seems to have been able to attain to human and ultra-human dimensions."

He does not mention the ant, but throughout his allusions the ant is continually being brought before my mind, in its sleepless activity, in its intelligence and social organisation, in its structure, and more particularly in the fact that it displays, in addition to the two forms, the male and the female form, that almost all other animals possess, a number of other sexless creatures, workers, soldiers, and the like, differing from one another in structure, character, power, and use, and yet all members of the same species. For these Selenites, also, have a great variety of forms. Of course, they are not only colossally greater in size than ants, but also, in Cavor's opinion at least, in intelligence, morality, and social wisdom are they colossally greater than men. And instead of the four or five different forms of ant that are found, there are almost innumerably different forms of Selenite. I had endeavoured to indicate the very considerable difference observable in such Selenites of the outer crust as I happened to encounter; the differences in size and proportions were certainly as wide as the differences between the most widely separated races of men. But such differences as I saw fade absolutely to nothing in comparison with the huge distinctions of which Cavor tells. It would seem the exterior Selenites I saw were, indeed, mostly engaged in kindred occupations – mooncalf herds, butchers, fleshers, and the like. But within the moon, practically unsuspected by me, there are, it seems, a number of other sorts of Selenite, differing in size, differing in the relative size of part to part, differing in power and appearance, and yet not different species of creatures, but only different forms of one species, and retaining through all their variations a certain common likeness that marks their specific unity. The moon is, indeed, a sort of vast ant-hill, only, instead of there being only four or five sorts of ant, there are many hundred different sorts of Selenite, and almost every gradation between one sort and another.

It would seem the discovery came upon Cavor very speedily. I infer rather than learn from his narrative that he was captured by the mooncalf herds under the direction of these other Selenites who "have larger brain cases (heads?) and very much shorter legs." Finding he would not walk even under the goad, they carried him into darkness, crossed a narrow, plank-like bridge that may have been the identical bridge I had refused, and put him down in something that must have seemed at first to be some sort of lift. This was the balloon – it had certainly been absolutely invisible to us in the darkness – and what had seemed to me a mere plank-walking into the void was really, no doubt, the passage of the gangway. In this he descended towards constantly more luminous caverns of the moon. At first they descended in silence – save for the twitterings of the Selenites – and then into a stir of windy movement. In a little while the profound blackness had made his eyes so sensitive that he began to see more and more of the things about him, and at last the vague took shape.

"Conceive an enormous cylindrical space," says Cavor, in his seventh message, "a quarter of a mile across, perhaps; very dimly lit at first and then brighter, with big platforms twisting down its sides in a spiral that vanishes at last below in a blue profundity; and lit even more brightly – one could not tell how or why. Think of the well of the very largest spiral staircase or lift-shaft that you have ever looked down, and magnify that by a hundred. Imagine it at twilight seen through blue glass. Imagine yourself looking down that; only imagine also that you feel extraordinarily light, and have got rid of any giddy feeling you might have on earth, and you will have the first conditions of my impression. Round this enormous shaft imagine a broad gallery running in a much steeper spiral than would be credible on earth, and forming a steep road protected from the gulf only by a little parapet that vanishes at last in perspective a couple of miles below.

"Looking up, I saw the very fellow of the downward vision; it had, of course, the effect of looking into a very steep cone. A wind was blowing down the shaft, and far above I fancy I heard, growing fainter and fainter, the bellowing of the mooncalves that were being driven down again from their evening pasturage on the exterior. And up and down the spiral galleries were scattered numerous moon people, pallid, faintly luminous beings, regarding our appearance or busied on unknown errands.

"Either I fancied it or a flake of snow came drifting down on the icy breeze. And then, falling like a snowflake, a little figure, a little man-insect, clinging to a parachute, drove down very swiftly towards the central places of the moon.

"The big-headed Selenite sitting beside me, seeing me move my head with the gesture of one who saw, pointed with his trunk-like 'hand' and indicated a sort of jetty coming into sight very far below: a little landing-stage, as it were, hanging into the void. As it swept up towards us our pace diminished very rapidly, and in a few moments, as it seemed, we were abreast of it, and at rest. A mooring-rope was flung and grasped, and I found myself pulled down to a level with a great crowd of Selenites, who jostled to see me.

"It was an incredible crowd. Suddenly and violently there was forced upon my attention the vast amount of difference there is amongst these beings of the moon.

"Indeed, there seemed not two alike in all that jostling multitude. They differed in shape, they differed in size, they rang all the horrible changes on the theme of Selenite form! Some bulged and overhung, some ran about among the feet of their fellows. All of them had a grotesque and disquieting suggestion of an insect that has somehow contrived to mock humanity; but all seemed to present an incredible exaggeration of some particular feature: one had a vast right fore-limb, an enormous antennal arm, as it were; one seemed all leg, poised, as it were, on stilts; another protruded the edge of his face mask into a nose-like organ that made him startlingly human until one saw his expressionless gaping mouth. The strange and (except for the want of mandibles and palps) most insect-like head of the mooncalf-minders underwent, indeed, the most incredible transformations: here it was broad and low, here high and narrow; here its leathery brow was drawn out into horns and strange features; here it was whiskered and divided, and there with a grotesquely human profile. One distortion was particularly conspicuous. There were several brain cases distended like bladders to a huge size, with the face mask reduced to quite small proportions. There were several amazing forms, with heads reduced to microscopic proportions and blobby bodies; and fantastic, flimsy things that existed, it would seem, only as a basis for vast, trumpet-like protrusions of the lower part of the mask. And oddest of all, as it seemed to me for the moment, two or three of these weird inhabitants of a subterranean world, a world sheltered by innumerable miles of rock from sun or rain, *carried umbrellas* in their tentaculate hands – real terrestrial-looking umbrellas! And then I thought of the parachutist I had watched descend.

"These moon people behaved exactly as a human crowd might have done in similar circumstances: they jostled and thrust one another, they shoved one another aside, they even clambered upon one another to get a glimpse of me. Every moment they increased in numbers, and pressed more urgently upon the discs of my ushers" – Cavor does not explain what he means by this – "every moment fresh shapes emerged from the shadows and forced themselves upon my astounded attention. And presently I was signed and helped into a sort of litter, and lifted up on the shoulders of strong-armed bearers, and so borne through the twilight over this seething multitude towards the apartments that were provided for me in the moon. All about me were eyes, faces, masks, a leathery noise like the rustling of beetle wings, and a great bleating and cricket-like twittering of Selenite voices…"

We gather he was taken to a "hexagonal apartment," and there for a space he was confined. Afterwards he was given a much more considerable liberty; indeed, almost as much freedom as one has in a civilised town on earth. And it would appear that the mysterious being who is the ruler and master of the moon appointed two Selenites "with large heads" to guard and study him, and to establish whatever mental communications were possible with him. And, amazing and incredible as it may seem, these two creatures, these fantastic men insects, these beings of other world, were presently communicating with Cavor by means of terrestrial speech.

Cavor speaks of them as Phi-oo and Tsi-puff. Phi-oo, he says, was about 5ft high; he had small slender legs about 18in. long, and slight feet of the common lunar pattern. On these balanced a little body, throbbing with the pulsations of his heart. He had long, soft, many-jointed arms ending in a tentacled grip, and his neck was many-jointed in the usual way, but exceptionally short and thick. His head, says Cavor – apparently alluding to some previous description that has gone astray in space – "is of the common lunar type, but strangely modified. The mouth has the usual expressionless gape, but it is unusually small and pointing downward, and the mask is reduced to the size of a large flat nose-flap. On either side are the little eyes.

"The rest of the head is distended into a huge globe and the chitinous leathery cuticle of the mooncalf herds thins out to a mere membrane, through which the pulsating brain movements are distinctly visible. He is a creature, indeed, with a tremendously hypertrophied brain, and with the rest of his organism both relatively and absolutely dwarfed."

In another passage Cavor compares the back view of him to Atlas supporting the world. Tsi-puff it seems was a very similar insect, but his "face" was drawn out to a considerable length, and the brain hypertrophy being in different regions, his head was not round but pear-shaped, with the stalk downward. There were also litter-carriers, lopsided beings, with enormous shoulders, very spidery ushers, and a squat foot attendant in Cavor's retinue.

The manner in which Phi-oo and Tsi-puff attacked the problem of speech was fairly obvious. They came into this "hexagonal cell" in which Cavor was confined, and began imitating every sound he made, beginning with a cough. He seems to have grasped their intention with great quickness, and to have begun repeating words to them and pointing to indicate the application. The procedure was probably always the same. Phi-oo would attend to Cavor for a space, then point also and say the word he had heard.

The first word he mastered was "man," and the second "Mooney" – which Cavor on the spur of the moment seems to have used instead of "Selenite" for the moon race. As soon as Phi-oo was assured of the meaning of a word he repeated it to Tsi-puff, who remembered it infallibly. They mastered over one hundred English nouns at their first session.

Subsequently it seems they brought an artist with them to assist the work of explanation with sketches and diagrams – Cavor's drawings being rather crude. He was, says Cavor, "a being with an active arm and an arresting eye," and he seemed to draw with incredible swiftness.

The eleventh message is undoubtedly only a fragment of a longer communication. After some broken sentences, the record of which is unintelligible, it goes on:-

"But it will interest only linguists, and delay me too long, to give the details of the series of intent parleys of which these were the beginning, and, indeed, I very much doubt if I could give in anything like the proper order all the twistings and turnings that we made in our pursuit of mutual comprehension. Verbs were soon plain sailing – at least, such active verbs as I could express by drawings; some adjectives were easy, but when it came to abstract nouns, to prepositions, and the sort of hackneyed figures of speech, by means of which so much is expressed on earth, it was like diving in cork-jackets. Indeed, these difficulties were insurmountable until to the sixth lesson came a fourth assistant, a being with a huge football-shaped head, whose *forte* was clearly the pursuit of intricate analogy. He entered in a preoccupied manner, stumbling against a stool, and the difficulties that arose had to be presented to him with a certain amount of clamour and hitting and pricking before they reached his apprehension. But once he was involved his pentetration was amazing. Whenever there came a need of thinking beyond Phi-oo's by no means limited scope, this prolate-headed person was in request, but he invariably told the conclusion to Tsi-puff, in order that it might be remembered; Tsi-puff was ever the arsenal for facts. And so we advanced again.

"It seemed long and yet brief – a matter of days – before I was positively talking with these insects of the moon. Of course, at first it was an intercourse infinitely tedious and exasperating, but imperceptibly it has grown to comprehension. And my patience has grown to meet its limitations, Phi-oo it is who does all the talking. He does it with a vast amount of meditative provisional 'M'm – M'm' and has caught up one or two phrases, 'If I may say,' 'If you understand,' and beads all his speech with them.

"Thus he would discourse. Imagine him explaining his artist.

" 'M'm – M'm – he – if I may say – draw. Eat little – drink little – draw. Love draw. No other thing. Hate all who not draw like him. Angry. Hate all who draw like him better. Hate most people. Hate all who not think all world for to draw. Angry. M'm. All things mean nothing to him – only draw. He like you...if you understand... New thing to draw. Ugly – striking. Eh?

" 'He' – turning to Tsi-puff – 'love remember words. Remember wonderful more than any. Think no, draw no –

227

remember. Say' – here he referred to his gifted assistant for a word – 'histories – all things. He hear once – say ever.'

"It is more wonderful to me than I dreamt that anything ever could be again, to hear, in this perpetual obscurity, these extraordinary creatures – for even familiarity fails to weaken the inhuman effect of their appearance – continually piping a nearer approach to coherent earthly speech – asking questions, giving answers. I feel that I am casting back to the fable-hearing period of childhood again, when the ant and the grasshopper talked together and the bee judged between them..."

And while these linguistic exercises were going on Cavor seems to have experienced a considerable relaxation of his confinement. "The first dread and distrust our unfortunate conflict aroused is being," he said, "continually effaced by the deliberate rationality of all I do."... "I am now able to come and go as I please, or I am restricted only for my own good. So it is I have been able to get at this apparatus, and, assisted by a happy find among the material that is littered in this enormous store-cave, I have contrived to despatch these messages. So far not the slightest attempt has been made to interfere with me in this, though I have made it quite clear to Phi-oo that I am signalling to the earth.

" 'You talk to other?' he asked, watching me.

" 'Others,' said I.

" 'Others,' he said. 'Oh yes. Men?'

"And I went on transmitting."

Cavor was continually making corrections in his previous accounts of the Selenites as fresh facts flowed upon him to modify his conclusions, and accordingly one gives the quotations that follow with a certain amount of reservation. They are quoted from the ninth, thirteenth, and sixteenth messages, and, altogether vague and fragmentary as they are, they probably give as complete a picture of the social life of this strange community as mankind can now hope to have for many generations.

"In the moon," says Cavor, "every citizen knows his place. He is born to that place, and the elaborate discipline of training and education and surgery he undergoes fits him at last so completely to it that he has neither ideas nor organs for any purpose beyond it. 'Why should he?' Phi-oo would ask. If, for example, a Selenite is destined to be a mathematician, his teachers and trainers set out at once to that end. They check any incipient disposition to other pursuits, they encourage his mathematical bias with a perfect psychological skill. His brain grows, or at least the mathematical faculties of his brain grow, and the rest of him only so much as is necessary to sustain this essential part of him. At last, save for rest and food, his one delight lies in the exercise and display of his facility, his one interest in its application, his sole society with other specialists in his own line. His brain grows continually larger, at least so far as the portions engaging in mathematics are concerned; they bulge ever larger and seem to suck all life and vigour from the rest of his frame. His limbs shrivel, his heart and digestive organs diminish, his insect face is hidden under its bulging contours. His voice becomes a mere stridulation for the stating of formulae; he seems deaf to all but properly enunciated problems. The faculty of laughter, save for the sudden discovery of some paradox, is lost to him; his deepest emotion is the evolution of a novel computation. And so he attains his end.

229

"Or, again, a Selenite appointed to be a minder of mooncalves is from his earliest years induced to think and live mooncalf, to find his pleasure in mooncalf lore, his exercise in their tending and pursuit. He is trained to become wiry and active, his eye is indurated to the tight wrappings, the angular contours that constitute a 'smart mooncalfishness.' He takes at last no interest in the deeper part of the moon; he regards all Selenites not equally versed in mooncalves with indifference, derision, or hostility. His thoughts are of mooncalf pastures, and his dialect an accomplished mooncalf technique. So also he loves his work, and discharges in perfect happiness the duty that justifies his being. And so it is with all sorts and conditions of Selenites – each is a perfect unit in a world machine...

"These beings with big heads, on whom the intellectual labours fall, form a sort of aristocracy in this strange society, and at the head of them, quintessential of the moon, is that marvellous gigantic ganglion the Grand Lunar, into whose presence I am finally to come. The unlimited development of the minds of the intellectual class is rendered possible by the absence of any body skull in the lunar anatomy, that strange box of bone that clamps about the developing brain of man, imperiously insisting 'thus far and no farther' to all his possibilities. They fall into three main classes differing greatly in influence and respect. There are the administrators, of whom Phi-oo is one, Selenites of considerable initiative and versatility, responsible each for a certain cubic content of the moon's bulk; the experts like the football-headed thinker, who are trained to perform certain special operations; and the erudite, who are the repositories of all knowledge. To the latter class belongs Tsi-puff, the first lunar professor of terrestrial languages. With regard to these latter, it is a curious little thing to note that the unlimited growth of the lunar brain has rendered unnecessary the invention of all those mechanical aids to brain work which have distinguished the career of man. There are no books, no records of any sort, no libraries or inscriptions. All knowledge is stored in distended brains much as the honey-ants of Texas store honey in their distended abdomens. The lunar Somerset House and the lunar British Museum Library are collections of living brains...

"The less specialised administrators, I note, do for the most part take a very lively interest in me whenever they encounter me. They will come out of the way and stare at me and ask questions to which Phi-oo will reply. I see them going hither and thither with a retinue of bearers, attendants, shouters, parachute-carriers, and so forth – queer groups to see. The experts for the most part ignore me completely, even as they ignore each other, or notice me only to begin a clamorous exhibition of their distinctive skill. The erudite for the most part are rapt in an impervious and apoplectic complacency, from which only a denial of their erudition can rouse them. Usually they are led about by little watchers and attendants, and often there are small and active-looking creatures, small females usually, that I am inclined to think are a sort of wife to them; but some of the profounder scholars are altogether too great for locomotion, and are carried from place to place in a sort of sedan tub, wabbling jellies of knowledge that enlist my respectful astonishment. I have just passed one in coming to this place where I am permitted to amuse myself with these electrical toys, a vast, shaven, shaky head, bald and thin-skinned, carried on his grotesque stretcher. In front and behind came his bearers, and curious, almost trumpet-faced, news disseminators shrieked his fame.

"I have already mentioned the retinues that accompany most of the intellectuals: ushers, bearers, valets, extraneous tentacles and muscles, as it were, to replace the abortive physical powers of these hypertrophied minds. Porters almost invariably accompany them. There are also extremely swift messengers with spider-like legs and 'hands' for grasping parachutes, and attendants with vocal organs that could well nigh wake the dead. Apart from their controlling intelligence these subordinates are as inert and helpless as umbrellas in a stand. They exist only in relation to the orders they have to obey, the duties they have to perform.

"The bulk of these insects, however, who go to and fro upon the spiral ways, who fill the ascending balloons and drop past me clinging to flimsy parachutes are, I gather, of the operative class. 'Machine hands,' indeed, some of these are in actual nature – it is not figure of speech, the single tentacle of the mooncalf herd is profoundly modified for clawing, lifting, guiding, the rest of them no more than necessary subordinate appendages to these important mechanisms, have enormously developed auditory organs; some whose work lies in delicate chemical operations project a vast olfactory organ; others again have flat feet for treadles with anchylosed joints; and others – who I have been told are glassblowers – seem mere lung-bellows. but every one of these common Selenites I have seen at work is exquisitely adapted to the social need it meets. Fine work is done by fined-down workers, amazingly dwarfed and neat. Some I could hold on the palm of my hand. There is even a sort of turnspit Selenite, very common, whose duty and only delight it is to apply the motive power for various small appliances. And to rule over these things and order any erring tendency there might be in some aberrant natures are the most muscular beings I have seen in the moon, a sort of lunar police, who must have been trained from their earliest years to give a perfect respect and obedience to the swollen heads.

"The making of these various sorts of operative must be a very curious and interesting process. I am very much in the dark about it, but quite recently I came upon a number of young Selenites confined in jars from which only the fore-limbs protruded, who were being compressed to become machine-minders of a special sort. The extended 'hand' in this highly developed system of technical education is stimulated by irritants and nourished by injection, while the rest of the body is starved. Phi-oo, unless I misunderstood him, explained that in the earlier stages these queer little creatures are apt to display signs of suffering in their various cramped situations, but they easily become indurated to their lot; and he took me on to where a number of flexible-minded messengers were being drawn out and broken in. It is quite unreasonable, I know, but such glimpses of the educational methods of these beings affect me disagreeably. I hope, however, that may pass off, and I may be able to see more of this aspect of their wonderful social order. That wretched-looking hand-tentacle sticking out of its jar seemed to have a sort of limp appeal for lost possibilities; it haunts me still, although, of course it is really in the end a far more humane proceeding than our earthly method of leaving children to grow into human beings, and then making machines of them.

"Quite recently, too – I think it was on the eleventh or twelfth visit I made to this apparatus – I had a curious light upon the lives of these operatives. I was being guided through a short cut hither, instead of going down the spiral, and by the quays to the Central Sea. From the devious windings of a long, dark gallery, we emerged into a vast, low cavern, pervaded by an earthy smell, and as things go in this darkness, rather brightly lit. The light came from a tumultuous growth of livid fungoid shapes – some indeed singularly like our terrestrial mushrooms, but standing as high or higher than a man.

" 'Mooneys eat these?' said I to Phi-oo.

" 'Yes, food.'

" 'Goodness me!' I cried; 'what's that?'

"My eye had just caught the figure of an exceptionally big and ungainly Selenite lying motionless among the stems, face downward. We stopped.

" 'Dead?' I asked. (For as yet I have seen no dead the moon, and I have grown curious.)

" '*No!*' exclaimed Phi-oo. 'Him – worker – no work to do. Get little drink then – make sleep – till we him want. What good him wake, eh? No want him walking about.'

" 'There's another!' cried I.

"And indeed all that huge extent of mushroom ground was, I found, peppered with these prostrate figures sleeping under an opiate until the moon had need of them. There were scores of them of all sorts, and we were able to turn over some of them, and examine them more precisely than I had been able to do previously. They breathed noisily at my doing so, but did not wake. One, I remember very distinctly: he left a strong impression, I think, because some trick the light and of his attitude was strongly suggestive of a drawn-up human figure. His fore-limbs were long, delicate tentacles – he was some kind of refined manipulator – and the pose of his slumber suggested a submissive suffering. No doubt it was a mistake for me to interpret his expression in that way, but I did. And as Phi-oo

234

rolled him over into the darkness among the livid fleshiness again I felt a distinctly unpleasant sensation, although as he rolled the insect in him was confessed.

"It simply illustrates the unthinking way in which one acquires habits of feeling. To drug the worker one does not want and toss him aside is surely far better than to expel him from his factory to wander starving in the streets. In every complicated social community there is necessarily a certain intermittency of employment for all specialised labour, and in this way the trouble of an 'unemployed' problem is altogether anticipated. And yet, so unreasonable are even scientifically trained minds, I still do not like the memory of those prostrate forms amidst those quiet, luminous arcades of fleshy growth, and I avoid that short cut in spite of the inconveniences of the longer, more noisy, and more crowded alternative."

"My alternative route takes me round by a huge, shadowy cavern, very crowded and clamorous, and here it is I see peering out of the hexagonal openings of a sort of honeycomb wall, or parading a large open space behind, or selecting the toys and amulets made to please them by the dainty-tentacled jewellers who work in kennels below, the mothers of the moon world – the queen bees, as it were, of the hive. They are noble-looking beings, fantastically and sometimes quite beautifully adorned, with a proud carriage, and, save for their mouths, almost microscopic heads.

"Of the condition of the moon sexes, marrying and giving in marriage, and of birth and so forth among the Selenites, I have as yet been able to learn very little. With the steady progress of Phi-oo in English, however, my ignorance will no doubt as steadily disappear. I am of opinion that, as with the ants and bees, there is a large majority of the members in this community of the neuter sex. Of course on earth in our cities there are now many who never live that life of parentage which is the natural life of man. Here, as with the ants, this thing has become a normal condition of the race, and the whole of such eplacement as is necessary falls upon this special and by no means numerous class of matrons, the mothers of the moon-world, large and stately beings beautifully fitted to bear the larval Selenite. Unless I misunderstand an explanation of Phi-oo's, they are absolutely incapable of cherishing the young they bring into the moon; periods of foolish indulgence alternate with moods of aggressive violence, and as soon as possible the little creatures, who are quite soft and flabby and pale coloured, are transferred to the charge of celibate females, women 'workers' as it were, who in some cases possess brains of almost masculine dimensions."

Just at this point, unhappily, this message broke off. Fragmentary and tantalising as the matter constituting this chapter is, it does nevertheless give a vague, broad impression of an altogether strange and wonderful world – a world with which our own may have to reckon we know not how speedily. This intermittent trickle of messages, this whispering of a record needle in the stillness of the mountain slopes, is the first warning of such a change in human conditions as mankind has scarcely imagined heretofore. In that satellite of ours there are new elements, new appliances, traditions, an overwhelming avalanche of new ideas, a strange race with whom we must inevitably struggle for mastery – gold as common as iron or wood...

# CHAPTER TWENTY-FIVE

## The Grand Lunar

The penultimate message describes, with occasionally elaborate detail, the encounter between Cavor and the Grand Lunar, who is the ruler or master of the moon. Cavor seems to have sent most of it without interference, but to have been interrupted in the concluding portion. The second came after an interval of a week.

The first message begins: "At last I am able to resume this – " it then becomes illegible for a space, and after a time resumed in mid-sentence.

The missing words of the following sentence are probably "the crowd." There follows quite clearly: "grew ever denser as we drew near the palace of the Grand Lunar – if I may call a series of excavations a palace. Everywhere faces stared at me – blank, chitinous gapes and masks, eyes peering over tremendous olfactory developments, eyes beneath monstrous forehead plates; and undergrowth of smaller creatures dodged and yelped, and helmet faces poised on sinuous, long-jointed necks appeared craning over shoulders and beneath armpits. Keeping a welcome space about me marched a cordon of stolid, scuttle-headed guards, who had joined us on our leaving the boat in which we had come along the channels of the Central Sea. The quick-eyed artist with the little brain joined us also, and a thick bunch of lean porter-insects swayed and struggled under the multitude of conveniences that were considered essential to my state. I was carried in a litter during the final stage of our journey. This litter was made of some very ductile metal that looked dark to me, meshed and woven, and with bars of paler metal, and about me as I advanced there grouped itself a long and complicated procession.

"In front, after the manner of heralds, marched four trumpet-faced creatures making a devastating bray; and then came squat, resolute-moving ushers before and behind, and on either hand a galaxy of learned heads, a sort of animated encyclopaedia, who were, Phi-oo explained, to stand about the Grand Lunar for purposes of reference. (Not a thing in lunar science, not a point of view or method of thinking, that these wonderful beings did not carry in their heads!) Followed guards and porters, and then Phi-oo's shivering brain borne also on a litter. Then came Tsi-puff in a slightly less important litter; then myself on a litter of greater elegance than any other, and surrounded by my food and drink attendants. More trumpeters came next, splitting the ear with vehement outcries, and then several big brains, special correspondents one might well call them, or historiographers, charged with the task of observing and remembering every detail of this epoch-making interview. A company of attendants, bearing and dragging banners and masses of scented fungus and curious symbols, vanished in the darkness behind. The way was lined by ushers and officers in caparisons that gleamed like steel, and beyond their line, so far as my eyes could pierce the gloom, the heads of that enormous crowd extended.

238

"I will own that I am still by no means indurated to the peculiar effect of the Selenite appearance, and to find myself, as it were, adrift on this broad sea of excited entomology was by no means agreeable. Just for a space I had something very like what I should imagine people mean when they speak of the 'horrors.' It had come to me before in these lunar caverns, when on occasion I have found myself weaponless and with an undefended back, amidst a crowd of these Selenites, but never quite so vividly. It is, of course, as absolutely irrational a feeling as one could well have, and I hope gradually to subdue it. But just for a moment, as I swept forward into the welter of the vast crowd, it was only by gripping my litter tightly and summoning all my will-power that I succeeded in avoiding an outcry or some such manifestation. It lasted perhaps three minutes; then I had myself in hand again.

"We ascended the spiral of a vertical way for some time, and then passed through a series of huge halls, dome-roofed and elaborately decorated. The approach to the Grand Lunar was certainly contrived to give one a vivid impression of his greatness. Each cavern one entered seemed greater and more boldly arched than its predecessor. This effect of progressive size was enhanced by a thin haze of faintly phosphorescent blue incense that thickened as one advanced, and robbed even the nearer figures of clearness. I seemed to advance continually to something larger, dimmer, and less material.

"I must confess that all this multitude made me feel extremely shabby and unworthy. I was unshaven and unkempt; I had brought no razor; I had a coarse beard over my mouth. On earth I have always been inclined to despise any attention to my person beyond a proper care for cleanliness; but under the exceptional circumstances in which I found myself, representing, as I did, my planet and my kind, and depending very largely upon the attractiveness of my appearance for a proper reception, I could have given much for something a little more artistic and dignified than the husks I wore. I had been so serene in the belief that the moon was uninhabited as to overlook such precautions altogether. As it was I was dressed in a flannel jacket, knickerbockers, and golfing stockings, stained with every sort of dirt the moon offered, slippers (of which the left heel was wanting), and a blanket, through a hole in which I thrust my head. (These clothes, indeed, I still wear.) Sharp bristles are anything but an improvement to my cast of features, and there was an unmended tear at the knee of my knickerbockers that showed conspicuously as I squatted in my litter; my right stocking, too persisted in getting about my ankle. I am fully alive to the injustice my appearance did humanity, and if by any expedient I could have improvised something a little out of the way and imposing I would have done so. But I could hit upon nothing. I did what I could with my blanket – folding it somewhat after the fashion of a toga, and for the rest I sat as upright as the swaying of my litter permitted.

"Imagine the largest hall you have ever been in, imperfectly lit with blue light and obscured by a gray-blue fog, surging with metallic or livid-gray creatures of such a mad diversity as I have hinted. Imagine this hall to end in an open archway beyond which is a still larger hall, and beyond this yet another and still larger one, and so on. At the end of the vista, dimly seen, a flight of steps, like the steps of Ara Coeli at Rome, ascend out of sight. Higher and higher these steps appear to go as one draws nearer their base. But at last I came under a huge archway and beheld the summit of these steps, and upon it the Grand Lunar exalted on his throne.

"He was seated in what was relatively a blaze of incandescent blue. This, and the darkness about him, gave him an effect of floating in a blue-black void. He seemed a small, self-luminous cloud at first, brooding on his sombre throne; his brain case must have measured many yards in diameter. For some reason that I cannot fathom a number of blue search-lights radiated from behind the throne on which he sat, and immediately encircling him was a halo. About him, and little and indistinct in this glow, a number of body-servants sustained and supported him, and overshadowed and standing in a huge semicircle beneath him were his intellectual subordinates, his remembrancers and computators and searchers and servants, and all the distinguished insects of the court of the moon. Still lower stood ushers and messengers, and then all down the countless steps of the throne were guards, and at the base, enormous, various, indistinct, vanishing at last into an absolute black, a vast swaying multitude of the minor dignitaries of the moon. Their feet made a perpetual scraping whisper on the rocky floor, as their limbs moved with a rustling murmur.

"As I entered the penultimate hall the music rose and expanded into an imperial magnificence of sound, and the shrieks of the news-bearers died away...

"I entered the last and greatest hall...

"My procession opened out like a fan. My ushers and guards went right and left, and the three litters bearing myself and Phi-oo and Tsi-puff marched across a shiny darkness of floor to the foot of the giant stairs. Then began a vast throbbing hum, that mingled with the music. The two Selenites dismounted, but

I was bidden remain seated – I imagine as a special honour. The music ceased, but not that humming, and by a simultaneous movement of ten thousand respectful heads my attention was directed to the enhaloed supreme intelligence that hovered above me.

"At first as I peered into the radiating glow this quintessential brain looked very much like an opaque, featureless bladder with dim, undulating ghosts of convolutions writhing visibly within. Then beneath its enormity and just above the edge of the throne one saw with a start minute elfin eyes peering out of the glow. No face, but eyes, as if they peered through holes. At first I could see no more than these two staring little eyes, and then below I distinguished the little dwarfed body and its insect-jointed limbs shrivelled and white. The eyes stared down at me with a strange intensity, and the lower part of the swollen globe was wrinkled. Ineffectual-looking little hand-tentacles steadied this shape on the throne...

"It was great. It was pitiful. One forgot the hall and the crowd.

"I ascended the staircase by jerks. It seemed to me that this darkly glowing brain case above us spread over me, and took more and more of the whole effect into itself as I drew nearer. The tiers of attendants and helpers grouped about their master seemed to dwindle and fade into the night. I saw that shadowy attendants were busy spraying that great brain with a cooling spray, and patting and sustaining it. For my own part, I sat gripping my swaying litter and staring at the Grand Lunar, unable to turn my gaze aside. And at last, as I reached a little landing that was separated only by ten steps or so from the supreme seat, the woven splendour of the music reached a climax and ceased, and I was left naked, as it were, in that vastness, beneath the still scrutiny of the Grand Lunar's eyes.

"He was scrutinising the first man he had ever seen...

"My eyes dropped at last from his greatness to the ant figures in the blue mist about him, and then down the steps to the massed Selenites, still and expectant in their thousands, packed on the floor below. Once again an unreasonable horror reached out towards me... And passed.

"After the pause came the salutation. I was assisted from my litter, and stood awkwardly while a number of curious and no doubt deeply symbolical gestures were vicariously performed for me by two slender officials. The encyclopaedic galaxy of the learned that had accompanied me to the entrance of the last hall appeared two steps above me and left and right of me, in readiness for the Grand Lunar's need, and Phi-oo's pale brain placed itself about half-way up to the throne in such a position as to communicate easily between us without turning his back on either the Grand Lunar or myself. Tsi-puff took up position behind him. Dexterous ushers sidled sideways towards me, keeping a full face to the Presence. I seated myself Turkish fashion, and Phi-oo and Tsi-puff also knelt down above me. There came a pause. The eyes of the nearer court went from me to the Grand Lunar and came back to me, and a hissing and piping of expectation passed across the hidden multitudes below and ceased.

"That humming ceased.

"For the first and last time in my experience the moon was silent.

"I became aware of a faint wheezy noise. The Grand Lunar was addressing me. It was like the rubbing of a finger upon a pane of glass.

"I watched him attentively for a time, and then glanced at the alert Phi-oo. I felt amidst these slender beings ridiculously thick and fleshy and solid; my head all jaw and black hair. My eyes went back to the Grand Lunar. He had ceased; his attendants were busy, and his shining superfices was glistening and running with cooling spray.

"Phi-oo meditated through an interval. He consulted Tsi-puff. Then he began piping his recognisable English – at first a little nervously, so that he was not very clear.

" 'M'm – the Grand Lunar – wishes to say – wishes to say – he gathers you are – m'm – men – that you are a man from the planet earth. He wishes to say that he welcomes you – welcomes you – and wishes to learn – learn, if I may use the word – the state of your world, and the reason why you came to this.'

"He paused. I was about to reply when he resumed. He proceeded to remarks of which the drift was not very clear, though I am inclined to think they were intended to be complimentary. He told me that the earth was to the moon what the sun is to the earth, and that the Selenites desired very greatly to learn about the earth and men. He then told me, no doubt in compliment also, the relative magnitude and diameter of earth and moon, and the perpetual wonder and speculation with which the Selenites had regarded our planet. I meditated with downcast eyes, and decided to reply that men too had wondered what might lie in the moon, and had judged it dead, little recking of such magnificence as I had seen that day. The Grand Lunar, in token of recognition, caused his long blue rays to rotate in a very confusing manner, and all about the great hall ran the pipings and whisperings and rustlings of the report of what I had said. He then proceeded to put to Phi-oo a number of inquiries which were easier to answer.

"He understood, he explained, that we lived on the surface of the earth, that our air and sea were outside the globe; the latter part, indeed, he already knew from his astronomical specialists. He was very anxious to have more detailed information of what he called this extraordinary state of affairs, for from the solidity of the earth there had always been a disposition regard it as uninhabitable. He endeavoured first to ascertain the extremes of temperature to which we earth beings were exposed, and he was deeply interested by my descriptive treatment of clouds and rain. His imagination was assisted by the fact that the lunar atmosphere in the outer galleries of the night side is not infrequently very foggy. He seemed inclined to marvel that we did not find the sunlight too intense for our eyes, and was interested in my attempt to explain that the sky was tempered to a bluish colour through the refraction of the air, though I doubt if he clearly understood that. I explained how the iris of the human eyes can contract the pupil and save the delicate internal structure from the excess of sunlight, and was allowed to approach within a few feet of the Presence in order that this structure might be seen. This led to a comparison of the lunar and terrestrial eyes. The former is not only excessively sensitive to such light as men can see, but it can also *see* heat, and every difference in temperature within the moon renders objects visible to it.

"The iris was quite a new organ to the Grand Lunar. For a time he amused himself by flashing his rays into my face and watching my pupils contract. As a consequence, I was dazzled and blinded for some little time...

"But in spite of that discomfort I found something reassuring by insensible degrees in the rationality of this business of question and answer. I could shut my eyes, think of my answer, and almost forget that the Grand Lunar has no face...

"When I had descended again to my proper place the Grand Lunar asked how we sheltered ourselves from heat and storms, and I expounded to him the arts of building and furnishing. Here we wandered into misunderstandings and cross-purposes, due largely, I must admit, to the looseness of my expressions. For a long time I had great difficulty in making him understand the nature of a house. To him and his attendant Selenites it seemed, no doubt, the most whimsical thing in the world that men should build houses when they might descend into excavations, and an additional complication was introduced by the attempt I made to explain that men had originally begun their homes in caves, and that they were now taking their railways and many establishments beneath the surface. Here I think a desire for intellectual completeness betrayed me. There was also a considerable tangle due to an equally unwise attempt on my part to explain about mines. Dismissing this topic at last in an incomplete state, the Grand Lunar inquired what we did with the interior of our globe.

"A tide of twittering and piping swept into the remotest corners of that great assembly when it was last made clear that we men know absolutely nothing of the contents of the world upon which the immemorial generations of our ancestors had been evolved. Three times had I to repeat that of all the 4000 miles of distance between the earth and its centre men knew only to the depth of a mile, and that very vaguely. I understood the Grand Lunar to ask why had I come to the moon seeing we had scarcely touched our own planet yet, but he did not trouble me at that time to proceed to an explanation, being too anxious to pursue the details of this mad inversion of all his ideas.

"He reverted to the question of weather, and I tried to describe the perpetually changing sky, and snow, and frost and hurricanes. 'But when the night comes,' he asked, 'is it not cold?'

"I told him it was colder than by day.

" 'And does not your atmosphere freeze?'

"I told him not; that it was never cold enough for that, because our nights were so short.

" 'Not even liquefy?'

"I was about to say 'No,' but then it occurred to me that one part at least of our atmosphere, the water vapour of it, does sometimes liquefy and form dew, and sometimes freeze and form frost – a process perfectly analogous to the freezing of all the external atmosphere of the moon during its longer night. I made myself clear on this point, and from that the Grand Lunar went on to speak with me of sleep. For the need of sleep that comes so regularly every twenty-four hours to all things is part also of our earthly inheritance. On the moon they rest only at rare intervals, and after exceptional exertions. Then I tried to describe to him the soft splendours of a summer night, and from that I passed to a description of those animals that prowl by night and sleep by day. I told him of lions and tigers, and here it seemed as though we had come to a deadlock. For, save in their waters, there are no creatures in the moon not absolutely domestic and subject to his will, and so it has been for immemorial years. They have monstrous water creatures, but no evil beasts, and the idea of anything strong and large existing 'outside' in the night is very difficult for them…"

The record is here too broken to transcribe for the space of perhaps twenty words or more.

"He talked with his attendants, as I suppose, upon the strange superficiality and unreasonableness of (man) who lives on the mere surface of a world, a creature of waves and winds, and all the chances of space, who cannot even unite to overcome the beasts that prey upon his kind, and yet who dares to invade another planet. During this aside I sat thinking, and then at his desire I told him of the different sorts of men. He searched me with questions. "And for all sorts of work you have the same sort of men. But who thinks? Who governs?'

"I gave him an outline of the democratic method.

"When I had done he ordered cooling sprays upon his brow, and then requested me to repeat my explanation conceiving something had miscarried.

" 'Do they not do different things, then?' said Phi-oo.

"Some, I admitted, were thinkers and some officials; some hunted, some were mechanics, some artists, some toilers. 'But *all* rule,' I said.

" 'And have they not different shapes to fit them to their different duties?'

" 'None that you can see,' I said, 'except perhaps, for clothes. Their minds perhaps differ a little,' I reflected.

" 'Their minds must differ a great deal,' said the Grand Lunar, 'or they would all want to do the same things.'

"In order to bring myself into a closer harmony with his preconceptions, I said that his surmise was right. 'It was all hidden in the brain,' I said; 'but the difference was there.

Perhaps if one could see the minds and souls of men they would be as varied and unequal as the Selenites. There were great men and small men, men who could reach out far and wide, men who could go swiftly; noisy, trumpet-minded men, and men who could remember without thinking..." The record is indistinct for three words.

"He interrupted me to recall me to my previous statements. 'But you said all men rule?' he pressed.

" 'To a certain extent,' I said, and made, I fear, a denser fog with my explanation.

"He reached out to a salient fact. 'Do you mean,' he asked, 'that there is no Grand Earthly?'

"I thought of several people, but assured him finally there was none. I explained that such autocrats and emperors as we had tried upon earth had usually ended in drink, or vice, or violence, and that the large and influential section of the people of the earth to which I belonged, the Anglo-Saxons, did not mean to try that sort of thing again. At which the Grand Lunar was even more amazed.

" 'But how do you keep even such wisdom as you have?' he asked; and I explained to him the way we helped our limited [a word omitted here, probably "brains"] with libraries of books. I explained to him how our science was growing by the united labours of innumerable little men, and on that he made no comment save that it was evident we had mastered much in spite of our social savagery, or we could not have come to the moon. Yet the contrast was very marked. With knowledge the Selenites grew and changed; mankind stored their knowledge about them and remained brutes – equipped. He said this... [Here there is a short piece of the record indistinct.]

"He then caused me to describe how we went about this earth of ours, and I described to him our railways and ships. For a time he could not understand that we had had the use of steam only one hundred years, but when he did he was clearly amazed. (I may mention as a singular thing, that the Selenites use years to count by, just as we do on earth, though I can make nothing of their numeral system. That, however, does not matter, because Phi-oo understands ours.) From that I went on to tell him that mankind had dwelt in cities only for nine or ten thousand years, and that we were still not united in one brotherhood, but under many different forms of government. This astonished the Grand Lunar very much, when it was made clear to him. At first he thought we referred merely to administrative areas.

" 'Our States and Empires are still the rawest sketches of what order will some day be,' I said, and so I came to tell him... [At this point a length of record that probably represents thirty or forty words is totally illegible.]

"The Grand Lunar was greatly impressed by the folly of men in clinging to the inconvenience of diverse tongues. 'They want to communicate, and yet not to communicate,' he said, and then for a long time he questioned me closely concerning war.

"He was at first perplexed and incredulous. 'You mean to say,' he asked, seeking confirmation, 'that you run about over the surface of your world – this world, whose riches you have scarcely begun to scrape – killing one another for beasts to eat?'

"I told him that was perfectly correct.

"He asked for particulars to assist his imagination. 'But do not ships and your poor little cities get injured?' he asked, and I found the waste of property and conveniences seemed to impress him almost as much as the killing. 'Tell me more,' said the Grand Lunar; 'make me see pictures. I cannot conceive these things.'

"And so, for a space, though something loath, I told him the story of earthly War.

"I told him of the first orders and ceremonies of war, of warnings and ultimatums, and the marshalling and marching of troops. I gave him an idea of manoeuvres and positions and battle joined. I told him of sieges and assaults, of starvation and hardship in trenches, and of sentinels freezing in the snow. I told him of routs and surprises, and desperate last stands and faint hopes, and the pitiless pursuit of fugitives and the dead upon the field. I told, too, of the past, of invasions and massacres, of the Huns and Tartars, and the wars of Mahomet and the Caliphs, and of the Crusades. And as I went on, and Phi-oo translated, and the Selenites cooed and murmured in a steadily intensified emotion.

"I told them an ironclad could fire a shot of a ton twelve miles, and go through 20ft of iron – and how we could steer torpedoes under water. I went on to describe a Maxim gun in action, and what I could imagine of the Battle of Colenso. The Grand Lunar was so incredulous that he interrupted the translation of what I had said in order to have my verification of my account. They particularly doubted my description of the men cheering and rejoicing as they went into (? battle).

" 'But surely they do not like it!' translated Phi-oo.

"I assured them men of my race considered battle the most glorious experience of life, at which the whole assembly was stricken with amazement.

" 'But what good is this war?' asked the Grand Lunar, sticking to his theme.

251

" 'Oh! as for *good!*' said I; 'it thins the population!'

" 'But why should there be a need – ?'...

"There came a pause, the cooling sprays impinged upon his brow, and then he spoke again."

At this point a series of undulations that have been apparent as a perplexing complication as far back as Cavor's description of the silence that fell before the first speaking of the Grand Lunar become confusingly predominant in the record. These undulations are evidently the result of radiations proceeding from a lunar source, and their persistent approximation to the alternating signals of Cavor is curiously suggestive of some operator deliberately seeking to mix them in with his message and render it illegible. At first they are small and regular, so that with a little care and the loss of very few words we have been able to disentangle Cavor's message; then they become broad and larger, then suddenly they are irregular, with an irregularity that gives the effect at last of some one scribbling through a line of writing. For a long time nothing can be made of this madly zigzagging trace; then quite abruptly the interruption ceases, leaves a few words clear, and then resumes and continues for all the rest of the message, completely obliterating whatever Cavor was attempting to transmit. Why, if this is indeed a deliberate intervention, the Selenites should have preferred to let Cavor go on transmitting his message in happy ignorance of their obliteration of its record, when it was clearly quite in their power and much more easy and convenient for them to stop his proceedings at any time, is a problem to which I can contribute nothing. The thing seems to have happened so, and that is all I can say. This last rag of his description of the Grand Lunar begins in mid-sentence.]

"…interrogated me very closely upon my secret. I was able in a little while to get to an understanding with them, and at last to elucidate what has been a puzzle to me ever since I realised the vastness of their science, namely, how it is they themselves have never discovered 'Cavorite.' I find they know of it as a theoretical substance, but they have always regarded it as a practical impossibility, because for some reason there is no helium in the moon, and helium – "

[Across the last letters of helium slashes the resumption of that obliterating trace. Note that word "secret," for on that, and that alone, I base my interpretation of the message that follows, the last message, as both Mr Wendigee and myself now believe it to be, that he is ever likely to send us.]

# CHAPTER TWENTY-SIX

## The Last Message Cavor Sent to the Earth

In this unsatisfactory manner the penultimate message of Cavor dies out. One seems to see him away there in the blue obscurity amidst his apparatus intently signalling us to the last, all unaware of the curtain of confusion that drops between us; all unaware, too, of the final dangers that even then must have been creeping upon him. His disastrous want of vulgar common sense had utterly betrayed him. He had talked of war, he had talked of all the strength and irrational violence of men, of their insatiable aggressions, their tireless futility of conflict. He had filled the whole moon world with this impression of our race, and then I think it is plain that he made the most fatal admission that upon himself alone hung the possibility – at least for a long time – of any further men reaching the moon. The line the cold, inhuman reason of the moon would take seems plain enough to me, and a suspicion of it, and then perhaps some sudden sharp realisation of it, must have come to him. One imagines him about the moon with the remorse of this fatal indiscretion growing in his mind. During a certain time I am inclined to guess the Grand Lunar was deliberating the new situation, and for all that time Cavor may have gone as free as ever he had gone. But obstacles of some sort prevented his getting to his electro-magnetic apparatus again after that message I have just given. For some days we received nothing. Perhaps he was having fresh audiences, and trying to evade his previous admissions. Who can hope to guess?

And then suddenly, like a cry in the night, like a cry that is followed by a stillness, came the last message. It is the briefest fragment, the broken beginnings of two sentences.

The first was: "I was mad to let the Grand Lunar know – "

There was an interval of perhaps a minute. One imagines some interruption from without. A departure from the instrument – a dreadful hesitation among the looming masses of apparatus in that dim, blue-lit cavern – a sudden rush back to it, full of a resolve that came too late. Then, as if it were hastily transmitted came: "Cavorite made as follows: take – "

There followed one word, a quite unmeaning word as it stands: "uless."

And that is all.

It may be he made a hasty attempt to spell "useless" when his fate was close upon him. Whatever it was that was happening about that apparatus we cannot tell. Whatever it was we shall never, I know, receive another message from the moon. For my own part a vivid dream has come to my help, and I see, almost as plainly as though I had seen it in actual fact, a blue-lit shadowy dishevelled Cavor struggling in the grip of these insect Selenites, struggling ever more desperately and hopelessly as they press upon him, shouting, expostulating, perhaps even at last fighting, and being forced backwards step by step out of all speech or sign of his fellows, for evermore into the Unknown – into the dark, into that silence that has no end...

# H G Wells

## The History of Mr Polly

Mr Polly is one of literature's most enduring and universal creations. An ordinary man, trapped in an ordinary life, Mr Polly makes a series of ill-advised choices that bring him to the very brink of financial ruin. Determined not to become the latest victim of the economic retrenchment of the Edwardian age, he rebels in magnificent style and takes control of his life once and for all.

ISBN 0-7551-0404-8

# H G WELLS

## IN THE DAYS OF THE COMET

Revenge was all Leadford could think of as he set out to find the unfaithful Nettie and her adulterous lover. But this was all to change when a new comet entered the earth's orbit and totally reversed the natural order of things. The Great Change had occurred and any previous emotions, thoughts, ambitions, hopes and fears had all been removed. Free love, pacifism and equality were now the name of the game. But how would Leadford fare in this most utopian of societies?

ISBN 0-7551-0406-4

# H G WELLS

## THE INVISIBLE MAN

On a cold wintry day in the depths of February a stranger
appeared in The Coach and Horses requesting a room. So
strange was this man's appearance, dressed from head to foot
with layer upon layer of clothing, bandages and the most
enormous glasses, that the owner, Mrs Hall, quite wondered
what accident could have befallen him. She didn't know then that
he was invisible – but the rumours soon began to spread…

H G Wells' masterpiece *The Invisible Man* is a classic science-
fiction thriller showing the perils of scientific advancement.

ISBN 0-7551-0407-2

# H G WELLS

## THE ISLAND OF DR MOREAU

A shipwreck in the South Seas brings a doctor to an island paradise. Far from seeing this as the end of his life, Dr Moreau seizes the opportunity to play God and infiltrate a reign of terror in this new kingdom. Endless cruel and perverse experiments ensue and see a series of new creations – the 'Beast People' – all of which must bow before the deified doctor.

Originally a Swiftian satire on the dangers of authority and submission, Wells' *The Island of Dr Moreau* can now just as well be read as a prophetic tale of genetic modification and mutability.

ISBN 0-7551-0408-0

# H G Wells

## Men Like Gods

Mr Barnstaple was ever such a careful driver, careful to indicate before every manoeuvre and very much in favour of slowing down at the slightest hint of difficulty. So however could he have got the car into a skid on a bend on the Maidenhead road?

When he recovered himself he was more than a little relieved to see the two cars that he had been following still merrily motoring along in front of him. It seemed that all was well – except that the scenery had changed, rather a lot. It was then that the awful truth dawned: Mr Barnstaple had been hurled into another world altogether.

How would he ever survive in this supposed Utopia, and more importantly, how would he ever get back?

ISBN 0-7551-0413-7

# H G WELLS

## THE WAR OF THE WORLDS

'No one would have believed in the last years of the nineteenth century that this world was being watched keenly and closely by intelligences greater than man's...'

A series of strange atmospheric disturbances on the planet Mars may raise concern on Earth but it does little to prepare the inhabitants for imminent invasion. At first the odd-looking Martians seem to pose no threat for the intellectual powers of Victorian London, but it seems man's superior confidence is disastrously misplaced. For the Martians are heading towards victory with terrifying velocity.

*The War of the Worlds* is an expertly crafted invasion story that can be read as a frenzied satire on the dangers of imperialism and occupation.

ISBN 0-7551-0426-9

HOUSE OF
STRATUS

Internet:    www.houseofstratus.com including synopses and features.

Email:       sales@houseofstratus.com
             info@houseofstratus.com
             (please quote author, title and credit card details.)

Tel:         Order Line
             0800 169 1780 (UK)
              800 724 1100 (USA)
             International
             +44 (0) 1845 527700 (UK)
             +01     845 463 1100 (USA)

Fax:         +44 (0) 1845 527711 (UK)
             +01     845 463 0018 (USA)
             (please quote author, title and credit card details.)

Send to:     House of Stratus Sales Department      House of Stratus Inc.
             Thirsk Industrial Park                 2 Neptune Road
             York Road, Thirsk                      Poughkeepsie
             North Yorkshire, YO7 3BX               NY 12601
             UK                                     USA